I0597995

# CONFESSION

EDWIN (EDDIE) ELFORD is a retired police sergeant who, as a rookie, found himself in the East End of London close to the famous Petticoat Lane. After service at several stations in the Metropolis, he had the chance to be an Instructor at Peel House and at Hendon. On leaving the Force, he became a teacher, then one of the managers of a leisure centre and, finally, spent 12 years in management in the Ministry of Defence.

**By the same author**

**A short story**

**'They can't box at Oxford'**

# CONFESSION

## Edwin Elford

Published in Great Britain by Edwin Elford

Printed and bound by Lulu

Copyright © 2008 Edwin Elford

ISBN  978-0-9559770-0-8

The right of Edwin Elford to be identified as the Author of the work has been asserted by him in accordance with the Copyright, Designs and Patents Act 1988


All rights reserved. No part of this publication may be reproduced, stored in a retrieval system, or transmitted in any form or by any means without the prior permission of the author, nor be otherwise circulated in any form of binding or cover other than that in which it is published and without similar conditions being imposed on the subsequent publisher.


All characters in this publication are fictitious and any resemblance to real persons, living or dead, is purely coincidental.

**To my late wife, Jean Iris**

My thanks to Richard Ellington and Stuart McClure for their help and also to Pasture Farm for permission to use the cover photograph.

# CHAPTER ONE

'No! Absolutely not!' Detective Sergeant Johnny Spencer almost shouted the words and they rang around the interview room. He glared at the Senior Officers of the Metropolitan Police Corruption Enquiry Board who were ranged around the long table in front of him. He glared particularly at Assistant Chief Constable Charles Perkins, whose most recent question to him had been a repetition of several that had gone before, although phrased differently. The thrust of all the questions, the steady repetition of which had got under his skin, was 'Did you and your colleague, Detective Chief Inspector Albert Thompson, take a bribe of £10,000 from the Steadman brothers, who are now in prison?'

Perkins had been assigned to the enquiry from the Hertfordshire Force and sat alongside Detective Chief Superintendent Tobin, from the same Force, and two young Inspectors from Surrey, there to do most of the leg work, and who, judging by their speech and appearance, were from the graduate intake.

It was Johnny's fate to have come before the Enquiry Board.

As he sat there, listening to his outburst ringing around the room, it occurred to him how quickly the human mind could work because, although it was only a few moments before Perkins uttered some placatory and at the same time admonitory words, there was time for his memory to hurtle over the whole history of how he came to be there. Beginning with the day when his Superintendent had called him into his office to face him with two grim-faced strangers who were identified as Inspectors from the enquiry team. He was told that, with his colleague DCI Thompson, he was suspected of taking a bribe, was cautioned and then cross-questioned for a couple of hours.

It ended with his being suspended from duty and having to clear his desk and take all his personal belongings out to his car, under the eyes of his friends and colleagues at the station.

Unknown to him, a similar procedure had taken place much earlier that day with his colleague Albert Thompson.

His suspension had lasted six months. Six months of idleness and worry, punctuated by a series of further interviews, during which his whole life had been trawled over and during which he had maintained his innocence doggedly - not difficult, because he knew it to be true. His confidence had, in a silly way, weakened in the face of the repeated allegations and what he knew must have been some nagging doubts in the minds of those who knew him. Doubts of the 'there's no smoke without fire' variety.

He had even wondered how strongly his wife Tracey, since divorced, believed in him, however often she said she did, and how much the suspension had contributed to the breakdown of his marriage.

During this time, similar interviews had been carried out with his colleague, always separately, and they had been warned not to contact one another.

It was a question from Perkins regarding Albert that brought Johnny back to reality. 'I see that you have worked with Thompson many times. How far back does your relationship with him go?'

'As you can see from the records, we have been a very successful team; the number of Commissioner's Commendations clearly indicates that' replied Johnny forcefully 'and both of us have unblemished records.'

Perkins nodded, saying 'Yes ... but it's how these results are obtained that sometimes gives reason for thought.'

Johnny's hackles rose 'Listen, these two villains, the Steadman brothers, who we put away, were ruling the roost in West London and were responsible for many crimes we couldn't prove. Their reputation was such that no-one would dare risk giving evidence against them.'

Perkins, again 'That may be so, but we're getting away from the reason that we're here - to answer the allegations of you both taking £10,000 – let's concentrate on that.'

'And I've told till I'm blue in the face, during all these interviews, that these allegations from two right villains are completely unfounded and untrue. They are obviously trying to create a smoke screen to get some time off their sentences - and that's the real reason that we're here today. Besides, do you honestly think that DCI Thompson and I would risk throwing away our pensions for a measly £5,000 each?'

'Police officers have been known to accept bribes of far less than that, haven't they?' commented Perkins 'And are you saying that if the bribe had been much larger you might have been tempted?'

'No, of course not, you're just trying to put words in my mouth, you must be getting desperate.' After getting that off his chest, Johnny sat back and looked questioningly around the table.

'Sergeant Spencer.' It was Perkins again. 'We have almost completed our enquiries and you will be hearing from us soon. Thank you for your attendance, you can go now.'

Johnny rose, nodded to the Board and, without another word, left the room, confident that Albert's interview earlier in the day would have ended in a similar fashion.

When he got outside, he was thankful that the interview was over but, at the same time, felt aggrieved that he had not had adequate support from Inspector Buller, his reporting officer at his station. There had been history between the two men going back over a number of years and they now hated one another.

Buller, the older of the two, was a strong character with a direct manner which he cultivated to conceal a lack of confidence. He could be tetchy, was easily hurt despite his bluster, but was ambitious where Spencer was not. He was jealous of Spencer, who was tall, good-looking and with an easy manner, and who seemed to get on with most people, whereas Buller had to impose himself strongly to get the same result.

\*\*\*\*\*\*

The following week saw Johnny and Albert called to their Superintendent's office to be told that the Board of Enquiry had decided that the allegations had been unfounded. One hurdle remained, namely another enquiry would have to be held to see if there had been any breaches of the Force's own Disciplinary Code. This duly took place and the result was the same. They were both reinstated immediately. After another visit to the Super's office they were congratulated once more and told that, as far as he was concerned, there had never been any doubt about the result and that they could always count on his support.

Their colleagues had gathered round in the canteen to give their congratulations and sympathy to Johnny and Albert and eventually they found themselves alone. It was then that Johnny told his colleague how badly he had been affected by the months of inactivity and that he intended to leave the Force. He also told him that during the suspension he had completed the 'Knowledge' and intended to be his own boss and become a black cab driver. The money he would get from the return of his pension contributions would go a long way towards the cost of a new London cab.

Albert was horrified. He couldn't believe that Johnny would leave the Force, because he was such a good copper and they had made such a good team together.

He was to be proved wrong in this belief.

# CHAPTER TWO

On the morning after his farewell party on leaving the Force, Albert drove Johnny to Gatwick Airport. Even at this late stage, he was still trying to persuade him to stay, but without success.

On the plane, Johnny smiled to himself as he recalled that it had been a very good farewell party, so much so that he then slept through most of the flight. A very smart DanAir stewardess wakened him just prior to landing by offering him a glass of cold, fresh orange juice, which he accepted gratefully. He slipped on a pair of sunglasses to protect his bloodshot eyes and looking out of the window saw the tarmac rushing up towards him as the plane homed in on the narrow landing strip of Corfu Airport. He could see clearly water on either side and green-covered hills in the distance. In no time the wheels bumped on the tarmac, the engine thrust into reverse, the plane gradually slowed and the white airport buildings came into view as the plane turned and taxied towards the point where it would disgorge its passengers.

Everywhere was bathed in brilliant sunshine, as if welcoming the visitors to the island. The landing lights inside the Boeing were extinguished and the passengers, whom Johnny had hardly noticed until now, unfastened their seat belts and began to retrieve their hand luggage from the compartments overhead. Johnny relaxed and remained seated, avoiding the mad scramble.

He was in no hurry, in fact he had all the time in the world. Eventually, however, he too collected his hand luggage, managed a brief smile and a few words of gratitude to the blonde stewardess and left the plane.

On his way down the steps the heat of the midday sun suddenly took effect and for a moment he clung to the handrail until his head stopped spinning. It had certainly been a good party.

Despite feeling rough, he found the heat pleasurable. It had been a long lousy summer in England and the prospect of guaranteed good weather for a few days appealed to him greatly.

After collecting his luggage, he made his way with the other passengers towards the Customs Hall. As he handed over his passport, the official drew the attention of a Greek police officer alongside him to the entry under 'Profession' which showed 'Detective Sergeant'. The officer's dark-skinned face broke into a smile, displaying a neat array of white teeth accentuated by his rich, black moustache.

'You have come for a holiday, Mr. Spencer?'

'Yes, a holiday' replied Johnny, returning the smile and nodding his head in agreement. The sympathetic bond which exists between the police of different countries was apparent in his friendly reception. Each appreciates the common problems encountered when dealing with difficult people from all walks of life.

'I hope you enjoy our island' said the official, handing back Johnny's passport. 'Thanks, I'm sure I will' replied Johnny and, picking up his luggage, he made his way through the cool airport lounge, up the stairs and into the large cafeteria and bar, which overlooked the airfield.

After downing a large brandy and two cups of black coffee, Johnny felt much better and anxious to be on his way. With a renewed bounce to his stride, he retraced his steps to the end of the airport hall and stopped outside the office of a car hire company.

'I have a car booked in the name of Spencer' he announced clearly to the attractive, uniformed Greek girl behind the counter. She ran a beautifully manicured red fingernail down the list in front of her and Johnny couldn't help inhaling her exquisite perfume. Noting such details led Johnny to conclude that he was recovering rapidly from his hangover. She also spoke near perfect English and he recalled that on his previous visit to the island, with his wife before the breakdown of his marriage, he had been amazed by the number of people of all ages on Corfu who spoke English. The reason was simple really. The elderly could still remember the old ties with British rule, the middle-aged found themselves connected with the tourist industry, in order to make a living, and the young all learned English as a second language at school. This fact, together with the natural friendliness of the Corfuotes was one of the main reasons for his returning to the island.

A yellow Fiat 125 screeched to a halt outside the building and a young dark-skinned Greek jumped out. Johnny checked the vehicle over with him, signed the necessary documents at the counter, threw his case and hand luggage into the back and, with a smile and a few words of thanks, was off.

Leaving the airport, he headed for Corfu Town and within minutes he was on the outskirts and driving through an old part of the town that had obviously seen better days. Corfu was busy, dusty, noisy and hot and he decided to get out of town as quickly as possible. Passing several crowded tavernas, with people sitting under brightly-coloured awnings, he was tempted to stop as the smell of food filled his nostrils. He smiled as he found himself following a carroza taking tourists around the town. The sight of the highly-painted cart with the huge shade and large wheels brought back memories of his last visit when with his wife he had enjoyed a similar trip around the town.

Soon he was clear of the town and heading north along the coast road on the east side of the island. The change in the landscape was dramatic, almost unreal. For such a hot climate it was amazingly green. The mountains in the centre of the island were covered with trees and in amongst them were conifers standing tall, like sentinels. As he drove along, the mountains stretched high towards the centre of the island whilst on his right, under a varied coastline, lay the beautiful, inviting blue sea.

The roads were remarkably good at this stage. Then, as he approached one of the many small villages, they became so unbelievably bad that it seemed they might have been purposely neglected in order to keep strangers away. Deep craters filled with loose stones greeted Johnny as he entered the village. Despite these hazards, huge fifty-seater coaches and buses squeezed their way through the tiny village where the coach sides almost scraped the houses. Inevitably there was much pulling into the side and backing up, accompanied by much shouting and waving of arms as the Greek drivers performed miracles with their huge vehicles.

It was as hot as hell in the car and the perspiration began to pour out of Johnny; eventually he found himself driving along a flat stretch of the road at a holiday resort called Ipsos. Here the road followed the water's edge and he could bear the heat no longer. Hangover or not, he had to get his head under that blue sea to cool off.

He was in luck for, suddenly, a parking spot appeared before him. Perhaps someone had left the beach to take their siesta. On the beach, only the hardened or the mad remained, braving the sun at its strongest. Within minutes, Johnny had changed into his trunks and was walking slowly into the warm blue sea. As the water deepened he plunged and remained face downwards for as long as he could hold his breath. It was glorious. He imagined that he could hear steam hissing as the water cooled his face, ears and head. The feeling of relief and sheer pleasure was indescribable.

Eventually he came up for air, shook his head, opened his eyes and, turning on to his back, he floated with his arms and legs in a star shape, audibly groaning with pleasure. For several minutes he indulged himself in this way, oblivious of anyone or anything.

Suddenly, considerably cooled down by now, he turned over and swam strongly away from the shore. After about 100 yards he stopped and took in a panoramic view of Ipsos. From this distance it was amazing how the scene changed. With the breathtaking addition of a backcloth of richly-wooded mountains, the picture was complete. What had just been a tree-lined road along the sea shore was transformed into a colourful scene of immense beauty.

Ipsos had served its purpose - Johnny was beginning to feel quite human again - but it was still far too busy, with too many teenagers around. Where he was heading it would be much quieter - there would be peace and time to think.

He swam to the shore, relaxed for a while until almost dry, and then dressed.

Along the front there were numerous tavernas, some even with English pub-style names, which he avoided. Eventually he sat down at a gaily-covered table in the shade and ordered a lager, his favourite drink. This would be no problem on Corfu as the three main beers on the island were all the lager type. The Amstel, which he had ordered, being a Dutch import and the other two were the German Henninger and the Greek Fix, all being very drinkable as far as Johnny was concerned.

When the waiter brought the ice-cold beer he took a long draught. It was good and refreshing. He relaxed and looked around him. The aroma of food from another table filled his nostrils and the smell was so inviting that eventually he gave in to temptation and ordered a huge plateful of delicious spaghetti. He expected that he would have a full meal when he reached his destination.

Leaving Ipsos much refreshed, Johnny headed along the coast road, always in a northerly direction. His thoughts turned to the reason for his visit to the island; basically it was to be the beginning of a new stage in his life.

Just over seven years earlier, at the age of thirty, he had left the Royal Marines and joined the Metropolitan Police in London. After the normal spell on the beat, he had shown an aptitude for plain clothes work and before long was transferred to the CID. Working long hours and studying hard, something which did not come easily to him, he had made it to Detective Sergeant. Unfortunately, like so many of his colleagues before him, working hard to establish a career, his marriage had been a casualty.

His wife, Tracey, and he had split up amicably, shared everything and gone their separate ways. He had bought a small flat in South London just prior to leaving the Force and hoped to make a fresh start, of which the visit to Corfu for a holiday was to be the beginning.

He felt good about his new occupation - driving a black cab. The freedom of the job appealed to him and he would be his own boss. He also had one great attribute which had helped him as a police officer and would now help him again. He had an almost photographic memory and his ability to remember names and places would make the task relatively easy for him.

Now, he wondered just how much Albert had suffered during this time when he had been wrapped up in his own interests. The worry of the allegations and suspension must have affected him as well, and those two bastards certainly had a lot to answer for.

At this stage he was abruptly called back from his reminiscences as he approached another small village where the traffic was held up again. Always heading north, he came eventually to the hotel that he had booked, which overlooked a delightful, sandy bay. Exactly as he had imagined it.

He settled down to seemingly endless days of sun, sea and sand. He found the 'Friendly Island' to be just that, with lively tavernas, Greek dancing and cheap food and wine, even if not very interesting. His evenings and nights had been long with plenty of company and he had enjoyed them to the full but, as with all good things, it came to an end and it became time to return to London.

On his reluctant return to Gatwick Airport there was a message posted up for him directing him to call at the Police Office. There, he received the sad news of his friend Albert's sudden death and that the funeral was to be held the following day.

He was completely shattered by the unexpected news.

## CHAPTER THREE

Johnny hated funerals and more than anything else he hated 'Service Funerals' with a full graveside burial, because they always choked him.

The sun broke briefly through the clouds as he stood bareheaded and motionless and his eyes, misty with a mixture of emotion and hate, watched the gleaming coffin containing his old colleague Albert Thompson lowered slowly into the ground.

The Minister's voice rose in prayer as he scattered a handful of soil down onto the highly polished surface.

'Ashes to ashes, dust to dust.'

The sound of small stones striking the coffin seemed to jerk Johnny out of his thoughts and he raised his eyes to the other side of the deep black hole. Christine Thompson, the widow, a frail-looking figure dressed completely in black, sobbed uncontrollably. She was supported on one side by her 18-year old son Richard and on the other by her 16-year old daughter Elizabeth. Relatives flanked them, and on Johnny's side stood the closest of Bert's colleagues, mainly CID, all come to pay their last respects.

Albert Thompson and he had worked closely together for the past three years and now, just two weeks after Johnny had left the Police Force, Albert was dead.

It was Christine's wish that Albert be buried in their local churchyard, just outside London on the borders of Surrey. She was a staunch churchgoer, partly because of her upbringing, her father having been a country minister, and partly because the ever-increasing demands on her husband of CID work had led her to devote herself more and more to her family and the church. Bert, on the other hand, hadn't been much of a churchgoer but had always supported his wife whenever possible in her church activities. He could arrange, with amazing alacrity, gifts for stalls at the bazaars and fetes, not to mention transport and labour if anything required to be moved in a hurry.

The service, attended by many senior officers, both uniform and CID, and colleagues of all ranks, had been particularly moving. The Minister in his address had referred to him as 'being a kind and generous man who would go out of his way to give help when needed'.

This was true, but Johnny also knew the other side of Bert, who could be hard and uncompromising. Generally, though, he was well thought of by most people, the exceptions being perhaps the numerous villains he had 'put away' during his career.

After the service, the coffin, draped in a Metropolitan Police flag, was carried slowly on the shoulders of his closest colleagues, through two files of uniformed police, to the graveside. Johnny mechanically took half a pace forward and stared down at the coffin below.

'Sorry, old mate, that I wasn't back in time to be one of the bearers' he whispered and, fully aware that it was the wrong time to make a rational decision, continued 'Bert, those two evil Steadman bastards will suffer for this - I promise!'

'What did you say, Johnny?' whispered Detective Sergeant Charlie Read who moved alongside. Johnny shook his head, without answering, still staring down at the shiny coffin.

The dulcet tones of the Minister brought the service to a close.

Christine and her family filed past the coffin, pausing briefly to pay their last respects. They shook hands with the Minister and thanked him for the sympathetic way he had conducted the service. He smiled, offered further words of comfort, and then Christine, still assisted by her son and daughter, led the procession slowly from the churchyard to the waiting cars.

The uniformed officers lined up and in turn paused at the graveside, turned smartly and saluted the coffin in respect for their departed colleague.

This was the part that Johnny hated most about Service funerals. He had been in some tight situations whilst serving both in the Royal Marines and during his police service and, in fact, he had the reputation of being a bit of a hard man - but this scene always got to him. He turned quickly and hurried away, almost catching up with Christine and the family and, on reaching the gate, he made his way immediately to his parked car. He just wanted to get away on his own, to somewhere quiet where he could think.

He had scarcely sat down and closed the door, when there was a knock on the driver's window. Looking up he saw that it was Charlie Read. He wound down the window. His friend looked flustered.

'Hang on a minute Johnny' he said anxiously 'I've got a message for you from Christine. She especially wants you to come round to the house.' He paused for a moment before demanding, impatiently 'Will you be coming then?'

'Sorry, Charlie, I just wanted to be alone for a while' Johnny said, adding apologetically 'Yes, yes - alright, tell her I'll call round later.'

Read nodded, satisfied that he had carried out Christine's request, and walked briskly away to join his waiting colleagues.

Alone again, Johnny repeated out loud the promise he had made at the graveside 'Those two Steadman bastards will pay for this - I promise.' He relaxed, just saying the words out loud made him feel better - although he hadn't a clue just what he intended doing.

Now with the funeral over, he sat in his car, alone with his thoughts, and wondered just how he could make the Steadmans pay for this.

At least he was no longer in the Force, which left him free to pursue whichever line of action he decided to take. That was a strange quirk of fate - especially since Albert had tried so hard to prevent him from leaving.

CHAPTER FOUR

When he got to his old friend's neat, well-cared for house, it was crowded with Albert's relatives and many of his ex-colleagues whom he had not seen since his own farewell party. They commented on how tanned and well he looked, but already the holiday on Corfu was being pushed from his mind as other, more serious, matters occupied his thoughts. He made polite conversation till an opportunity presented itself to speak to Christine alone.

'Was there something special you wanted to see me about, Chris?' he asked, after offering his sympathies.

'Yes, there was Johnny' replied Christine 'I don't know whether it's important or not, but when Bert had his heart attack and was in intensive care, all wired up to one of those machines, I stayed with him through the night. At one stage he seemed to rally, he grabbed my arm tightly and in a weak voice said "Tell Johnny - Steadmans - the early days - confess." That was all he said and then he collapsed back again.'

She paused, as if painfully reliving the event 'Not long after that he died.'

Her eyes filled with tears as emotion engulfed her. Johnny comforted her as best he could and then she blurted out 'What does it mean, Johnny?'

'I really don't know, love' he replied 'At this moment it doesn't seem to make much sense. Are you sure that's exactly what he said?'

'Well, he was speaking very faintly at the time but I do remember quite distinctly what he said, and it was "Tell Johnny - Steadmans - the early days - confess"' she repeated and then continued, with concern showing on her lined face 'The Steadmans, weren't they the ones who made the allegations which led to you both being suspended?'

'Yes, that's right, but don't you worry any more about it. I'll give it some thought and if I can make some sense of it, I'll let you know. Alright?'

'Oh Johnny, you will keep in touch won't you?' she grabbed his arm tightly 'Albert thought such a lot of you.'

'Yes, I know love, and I can never repay all the things he did for me. How are the Police looking after you?' he asked, to change the subject.

'Very well, actually, everyone has been very kind. They say I shouldn't have any immediate financial problems, what with the police insurance cover, so that's a relief. But really, I haven't had time to think of the future - I just wanted to get today over first.'

'I'll come and see you in a couple of days' said Johnny 'and in the meantime if you need any help call me at this new number or get me through Charlie Read, if I'm out with the cab'. He handed her a piece of paper with his new address and telephone number, adding 'And also if you need a cab, lady, don't hesitate to give me a ring.'

'Thanks very much. I hope your new venture goes well. Albert was convinced you wouldn't make the break - he said you were too good a copper.'

'Yes – well - only time will tell whether or not it was a wise move.'

With that, he said his goodbyes to Christine and his colleagues, refusing the offers of company - he wanted to be alone.

Outside the house he decided to walk. Leaving the car parked where it was, he strode out, oblivious of people. He had had enough of death for one day and it was good to be on the move again with the slight breeze feeling good on his bronzed face. As he walked, he turned over in his mind the events of the last few hours and particularly the message from Albert. It just didn't make any sense. Maybe it was just the ramblings of a dying man - maybe Christine in her anxious state had mistaken what he had actually said - that he could well understand. One thing was certain though - he had mentioned the Steadmans and this convinced Johnny more that ever that they were partly to blame for his death.

He shook his head 'I'll give my full attention to Albert's words later' he said quietly to himself. What he really wanted to concentrate on was the immediate future and how he could avenge his friend's death - how he could make things awkward for the Steadmans, who were due out of prison soon, without them knowing.

The brisk walk, with the sheer physical pleasure of the exercise, was so much a part of his make up that it helped him to think and slowly a plan formed in his mind.

Then, feeling more settled, mentally and physically, he made his way back to his car and headed for home. Home? This was now the small flat had moved into, just prior to leaving for Corfu, and it was still in a mess. Suitcases and boxes remained unopened and he had imagined himself settling in at a leisurely pace, with no one to consider or worry about but himself. How wrong he had been! Now his whole world had turned upside down.

He eased the car to a halt outside the small, modern block of flats which stood back from the road in pleasant surroundings. The lush green lawns were well kept and complemented by several well-established trees which, thankfully, the planners had left standing and had built around. The varying green aspect was one of the main reasons why he had chosen this block and now the pleasing sight seemed to confirm his choice.

As he entered his flat, the smell of whisky greeted him and he wrinkled his nose.

Reaching out, he touched the half-empty bottle of duty-free Scotch standing on a small table with an empty glass beside it. He remembered clearly the previous evening when, on his return, after hearing of Albert's death, he had felt so alone and so full of remorse that he had turned to the then full bottle for comfort.

He looked at it now and toyed with the idea of having a snort, but changed his mind. He wanted to keep a clear head for the big day tomorrow, when he would take delivery of a black London taxicab worth thousands of pounds and put himself well into debt with the finance company. But, looking on the brighter side, it was also the beginning of a new phase of his life and the day when he would start earning again.

The next few days were hectic as Johnny, very much a new boy in the taxi business, tackled his new way of life enthusiastically. Other ex-coppers, also cabbies, helped him out greatly, teaching him the ropes, the shortcuts, which enabled him to settle down quickly. He enjoyed the freedom of being his own boss, able to work when it suited him, accountable to no one other than his customers and the fairly strict conditions of his cabby's licence. In addition, he had been very lucky to acquire a lockup garage in a quiet mews not far from the flat.

Early one morning, he had taken the cab 'up West' and struck lucky with his first fare from one of the hotels. It was a trip to Heathrow Airport.

The fare was a businessman who was on his way to a conference in New York and he was pleasant and generous with his tip.

Still feeling very much the new boy, Johnny joined the long feeder rank and, after taking the opportunity to grab some breakfast, he met the other cabbies - a sharp, voluble, friendly bunch.

When he finally reached the front of the line, some fifty minutes later, he struck lucky again with a run to the Hilton Hotel back in town, with three wealthy Americans dripping with gold and luggage in the back. It was their first visit to London and they were appreciative of his knowledgeable help and advice about which places to visit and which to avoid. They were also very generous with the tip, so he took a break and after a light lunch he was back in the cab again. This time, however, he didn't switch on the 'For Hire' sign and headed due south through Thornton Heath towards Croydon, away from the areas of London where he was best known.

Soon he was being overshadowed by the tall buildings which dominate the Croydon skyline, where the new buildings were gradually squeezing out the old. He went up through the underpass and on his left saw the Fairfield Halls and the Ashcroft Theatre. Once majestic looking, these were now also dwarfed by tall office blocks. The sight of the Halls brought back memories of concerts and plays he had enjoyed with his wife, Tracey, in happier times when the variety of entertainment presented and the efficiency of operation of both the Halls and the Theatre had never ceased to amaze him.

However, it was neither concert nor theatre that had brought him here now and at a suitable spot, well past the new Croydon Police Station, he stopped and picked up a fare.

This one was small, in his sixties, and dapper, in an old-fashioned way. His hair was smoothed down flat and he obviously took a pride in his appearance because, although his light pin-striped suit was a little loud, it was clean and well pressed. His face and particularly his nose were pink and blotchy - the sure sign of a drinker.

Anyone watching would have noticed two unusual things about the pick up. One was that the fare did not flag the cab down, nor did he give any instructions as to the destination. Obviously the driver was in charge.

Taxi and fare continued down the Brighton Road to Coulsdon, where it turned off right into Chipstead Valley Road. Soon the value of property moved up several brackets in the price range as they were among large detached houses facing green hilly fields. At the first convenient spot, Johnny pulled into a side road and parked.

He turned, slid the dividing glass partition back, and said cheerfully 'Well, Smithy boy, it's nice to see you again - quite like old times. How are they treating you?'

'Not often enough, Mr. Spencer' coughed the fare. He had lit a cigarette, the smoke from which was playing hell with his lungs.

Johnny waited patiently until the fit of coughing had ended 'Still trying to kill yourself with those fags are you? I thought you'd been warned off.'

'One of my few pleasures left now, a fag, and a glass of scotch' he spluttered and, quickly changing the painful subject of his health, he wheezed 'But what's up with you Mr. S? I fort you'd left the job. I was very surprised to get a bell from you after all this time - you ain't gone private 'ave you?'

'No Smithy, you're right. I have left the job and I haven't gone private.' He paused 'Smithy, it's rather personal - very personal' he added seriously.

This time Smithy drew hard on his cigarette and waited patiently as Johnny continued 'I've got a score to settle and I need your kind of help.'

'Well, we always got on alright before, didn't we?'

'Yes we did' agreed Johnny 'but this is a bit different'.

'Go on then' Smithy wheezed 'the suspense is bleedin' killing me.'

Johnny hesitated again, wondering how much he could take Smithy into his confidence. As snouts went, he was as reliable as any and they had built up a good working relationship over the years. In fact, several of Johnny's Commissioner's Commendations were really down to Smithy, but he had his weaknesses and one of them was scotch - the dreaded tongue loosener.

'I'll come straight to the point - you know the Steadman brothers?'

'Who the bleedin' 'ell doesn't?' interjected Smithy 'That was the finest job we ever did putting those bastards away' he smiled, showing uneven nicotine-stained teeth.

Undaunted by the horrible sight, Johnny continued 'Well, the crafty bastards managed to keep their noses clean while they were inside and they're due out soon with full remission.'

'Stitched up other poor sods to take the rap for them, you mean. I can't see them not running things in the nick.' He burst into another fit of coughing, the pink of his face turned to deep red and his eyes bulged. This time he looked anxiously at a spotted handkerchief he held to his mouth.

'That cough will be the bloody death of you yet, Smithy' said Johnny, when he had calmed down.

'I know, I know' replied Smithy irritably, and then he blurted out 'What's it you really want me to do?'

Johnny eased forward, looked into his pale watering eyes and whispered softly 'I want you to stir things up for the Steadmans so that they don't have it all their own way when they come out.'

'Christ Mr. S, that could be very dodgy.' Smithy paused, his brain working overtime, and finally he said 'I like the idea. As you know, I've got no time for those bastards - but 'ow the 'ell am I gonna do it?'

'Just think, who took over after the brothers went inside?'

'Well, after the towrags had sorted each other out it was the Mills mob, but they're inside now. I suppose it's got to be my Guvnor Terry Dace and his brother-in-law Poxy Huston and not forgetting that evil bastard Tommy Stock.'

'That's right' agreed Johnny enthusiastically 'so they won't be looking forward to the brothers coming back, will they?'

'No, not after the last spot of bother they 'ad when the Steadmans tried to put one over Dacey with that betting ring.'

Johnny paused and then asked the $64,000 question 'What I want you to do, Smithy, is to put the word about quietly that the brothers are boasting inside, that they can't wait to sort out Dace's lot and take over again.'

Smithy pursed his lips, drew in air noisily and shook his head 'You crafty bugger, Mr. S. Christ, then the shit would really hit the fan.'

Johnny waited patiently as the full effect of his suggestion sank in.

'But do you think you can do it safely, Smithy, and without anyone being able to trace it back to you - or me?'

Smithy's blotchy face had paled slightly and the muscles at the bottom of his jaw worked anxiously as he ground his back teeth together. His eyes darted from side to side as he answered 'Christ, Mr. S, it won't be easy, but I think I could manage it.' He lit another cigarette and Johnny noticed that his hands shook as he applied the flame to the tip. His slim hands were normally white-gloved and worked with amazing skill and dexterity, as they relayed the odds from the ring to his employer Terry Dace, the bookmaker.

Johnny broke the silence 'I'll make it worth your while' he offered encouragingly.

'We never 'ad no problems about the price before.' Then, as if he had had second thoughts about where the money was coming from, Smithy asked 'But 'ow're you making out at this lark?' as he looked around the inside of the brand new cab. 'This must have set you back a right packet.'

'Don't worry about the money. I've got enough to cover this job. The point is, will you do it?'

Johnny held his breath, watching Smithy's face intently. At last, after what seemed like ages, he heaved a sigh and replied in a resigned voice 'It would be a change I suppose - spreading the word instead of giving it. It shouldn't be any problem really' continued Smithy 'I could put the word round at the Dogs, or one of the race tracks, so that way it'll get back to them from someone else. It's a case of pickin' the right time and place.' He was silent for a moment and then said, reassuringly 'But you leave that side of it to me Mr. S, I'll sort something out.'

'Thanks Smithy, I knew I could rely on you. Sorry I can't put you further in the picture.'

'OK, but no doubt you've got your reasons and maybe it's better if I don't know anyway.'

He reached for another cigarette and Johnny turned, started the engine, completed a U-turn and headed back the way they had come.

CHAPTER FIVE

Claire Steadman raised the coloured celluloid shutters, allowing bright sunlight to enter the little florist shop in Clapham. The beauty and fragrance of the masses of different flowers were some consolation for having to manage the shop most of the day on her own.

How she had been spawned by the same parents as her dreaded brothers was one of those inexplicable quirks of nature. She couldn't have been more different. She was not too tall, 27 years old, shapely and attractive and with dark hair and brown eyes. Her generous mouth formed easily into a ready smile and this, together with a fine sense of humour, made her very popular with her customers.

From a young child she had been the good one of the family. While her brothers were serving their apprenticeships, in and out of various London juvenile courts and Borstal institutions, Claire had managed to win a scholarship to a good girls' school in South London. Always bright and quick witted, though not academic, she had later attended a secretarial college and taken a Higher National Diploma in Business Studies. In no time her ability and personality had led to a post as Personal Assistant to the Managing Director of a travel company and, for a while, life had been stable and good.

Meanwhile, her brothers Vic and Billy had been in and out of prison, sometimes separately, but as they were very much a team, usually together. Before they had become notorious, they often helped their father, Robert, run his fruit and veg business in the market, until the day arrived when they considered it beneath them to work on a stall. Eventually, their activities became more organised and their reputations grew until their strongarm tactics were feared throughout West London. Then, they no longer acknowledged their father's stall in the market.

Their mother Maisie had died when Claire was a teenager and she had no doubt that the worry caused by the brothers' lifestyle had been the biggest contributory factor, for which Claire could never forgive them.

Then, four years earlier, the two brothers had been put away for armed robbery.

Old Bobby Steadman had reached the stage in his life when he was too old to run the market stall every day and Claire, naturally enough, had refused to carry it on. However, the old man had worked hard all his life and had to have something to occupy him, for part of the day at least. With her good business sense, Claire had come up with the idea of the florist shop, which she saw as both a chance for her to become independent and also to help her father, whom she loved dearly, to ease gently into retirement.

As he was used to rising early and driving up to Covent Garden for the fruit and veg, it only meant a switch to flowers. He could continue to see all his old friends and give him a reason for living.

The florist shop had been a great success from the start and the combination of father and daughter had worked well. This phase of Claire's life, with her brothers in prison, had been the most stable that she could remember and only one thing seemed likely to spoil it. The brothers were due to come out of prison soon and Claire lived in dread of this. She had tried many times to persuade her father to emigrate with her to New Zealand or Australia, in order to make a fresh start away from her brothers, but he would not be budged. Understandably, he wanted to spend his remaining days with his lifelong friends and he claimed he was too old to start all over again.

She also knew that when her brothers did come out, they would continue their villainous activities, since they were both hardened criminals, who knew no other way of life. They might be more careful for a while but, as time went by, the chances they took to acquire or enhance their reputations would become greater and the odds against them being caught shorter.

They were a pair of evil bastards and she hated their guts. She hated them for what they were and for what they had done to her parents and herself. She was also determined that they were not going to get their hands on the quite reasonable profit from the little florist shop, which was entirely due to the efforts of herself and her father.

She had prepared two sets of business accounts. The first, the official one, was drawn up by her accountant for the Inland Revenue and kept at the bank and the second set, which was kept in the filing cabinet in the little office at the rear of the shop, showed the business as just ticking over and was the one to be shown to the brothers.

She didn't know how long it would take them to realise that the business was more prosperous than it appeared from this second set, but she would worry about that later.

Despite her gloomy thoughts about her brothers, she sang quietly as she arranged the beautiful flowers, whose wonderful fragrance filled the small shop. She was so engrossed in her pleasant task that she failed to hear the door open and someone enter, and she was startled when a man's voice said pleasantly 'You seem happy in your work, love.'

She was so surprised that she dropped the flowers she was unpacking and they splayed out on the floor at her feet. Regaining her composure quickly, she answered 'I am happy. Actually I was miles away, you startled me that's all' and looked into the smiling, mischievous eyes of the unfamiliar face before her, which was deeply tanned and topped by dark, curly hair.

'I'm sorry. Here, let me pick them up' said the man, showing his even, white teeth. Claire stood there flushed for the moment, as her heart settled down from the fright.

'No, really it's alright' she mumbled faintly, but by then it was too late as he was already on his knees retrieving the flowers.

She couldn't fail to notice the broad back and the rounded muscles beneath the white t-shirt and she just had time to think 'He looks rather dishy' when he stood up facing her and with a slight bow from his waist presented her with the flowers, saying 'Actually, I rather like these.' They were deep red carnations with long stems.

She had recovered her composure by now and the business woman in her came to the fore. 'Well, you couldn't buy flowers any fresher. I was just unpacking them as you spoke. I didn't hear you come in.'

'Yes, I'm sorry I startled you' he apologised again.

'That's alright. Do you really want the flowers?'

'Please - and put with them some of those lighter-coloured ones for contrast.'

Claire wrapped the flowers carefully, acutely aware of the mischievous eyes watching her every movement - admiringly, if her intuition was right.

She handed the flowers to him, rang the money in the till and with a cheerful 'Thanks and call again' watched him leave the shop. Curious about the attractive stranger, she moved forward amongst the flowers in the window and saw him get behind the wheel of a black cab and drive away. 'Oh, he's a cabby' she said out loud and then wondered why, when she called the rank for a cab, the driver was never one who looked like him.

Unknown to her, Johnny Spencer had been keeping the florist shop under casual observation for the past few days. Whenever he found himself in the area with a fare, he would drive past and was already acquainted with her habit of calling a cab from the rank in order to go to the local bank with her takings. He had already decided to follow up his campaign against the brothers through their sister, but after this first encounter he was having misgivings, since she had seemed such a pleasant person and certainly not what he had expected. In the end he decided that, as she was the only direct contact he could establish with the family, he would continue undeterred.

Consequently the following Friday lunchtime found him parked outside the shop in such a position that he could keep the telephone in full view. He reckoned that she was bound to go to the bank on Friday in order to leave as little cash as possible in the safe over the weekend and his guess was also that she would try to avoid the lunchtime queues at the bank. Her father had arrived earlier and he could see both of them inside the shop. He put on his Corfu sunglasses and pulled a cap down level with them. He had to be careful because it was just possible that the father had been present at his sons' trial and might recognise him.

When it was approaching 2 pm he concentrated. Surely, she must ring soon. Then he saw that she had picked up the phone and was dialling. He started up the cab and drove slowly around the block, in order to approach the shop from the direction of the rank, and a few minutes later he pulled up outside.

'That was quick - you must have been sitting on the phone' quipped Claire, as she entered the cab carrying six heavy bags of cash and, dumping them noisily on the floor, she closed the door behind her and said cheerfully 'To the bank, as usual' looking at the back of the driver's head, without recognising him.

'Must be a new driver on the rank' she thought, as the cab sped away from the shop. As she settled back, she looked at the reflection of his face in the inside mirror and began to think that it was familiar.

'Barclays in the High Street, isn't it?' the driver asked, without looking round.

'Yes, that's right' replied Claire, wondering this time whether the voice was familiar, along with those shoulders and black, curly hair sticking out from under the cap.

Johnny could see her scrutinising his face in the mirror, but he was concentrating more on the cab which was pulling up outside the shop just as they turned the corner at the other end of the street. Some cabby was about to be most annoyed that someone else had just pinched his fare. He put his foot down, thinking that was too bad - no doubt a similar thing would happen to him sometime in the future.

As he pulled up outside the bank, Claire called out 'Wait for me, will you?'

'Certainly lady, it will be a pleasure' came the reply, adding 'Can I give you a hand with those bags?' This time he turned round and, with a quickening of her heartbeat, Claire thought 'It's him!'

'Er no. I can manage, thanks' replied Claire, slightly flustered and annoyed at the way she felt. Her usual calm manner was disturbed by this stranger and, as she dismounted quickly with the bags and entered the bank, she could feel his eyes following her every step.

She approached the counter with the bags and, while the cash was being counted by the young, bespectacled clerk, her thoughts turned to the cabby waiting outside. 'Who is he?' she wondered 'He certainly is dishy but he doesn't seem like an ordinary cabbie. It's probably just a coincidence – he's just a new cabby on the rank, that's all.'

'Anything else, Miss Steadman' the bank clerk repeated loudly. She shook herself and, slightly embarrassed, replied 'No - no, that's all thank you. Sorry, I was deep in thought.' She could feel the colour coming to her cheeks as the young man smiled and handed back the bags and the paying-in book.

Johnny turned round and smiled as she entered the cab. 'Where to now' he asked cheerfully.

'We've met before, haven't we?' she demanded, ignoring the question. 'You remember me, then' said Johnny, in mock surprise.

'Of course I do.'

'That's good.'

'Why?'

'Well, you might have refused an invitation to dinner tonight from a complete stranger.'

'Oh, I see' replied Claire, colouring slightly and amazed and annoyed to find her heart beating just that bit faster. She continued 'You've certainly got a nerve.'

'What are the chances then?' persisted Johnny, looking into her dark eyes.

'I'll consider it on the way back to the shop' she replied sharply, knowing full well what her answer would be, but not wishing to appear too anxious. There was something she liked about this pleasant, rugged stranger and he seemed so different from her usual cabbies.

She was a good-looking girl and rarely short of male company, but somehow her relationships tended to be brief, her men usually disappearing quickly from the scene when they discovered, often from well-intentioned friends, who her brothers were.

Within minutes they were back outside the shop. Claire got down from the cab and handed over a £5 note, saying seriously 'Keep the change' and then her voice changed as she added casually 'The name's Claire and you can meet me here at seven if you like.'

'It'll be my pleasure, Claire, and they call me Johnny' he replied and jokingly touched his cap.

She smiled, turned and flounced into the shop.

Johnny put the cab into gear and pulled away, satisfied that his tactics were going according to plan. Contact had been established and, although what he was about to do was hardly ethical, it was necessary in order to penetrate the Steadman family circle. He smiled to himself as he thought of Claire - so bright, with her trim figure and good looks - maybe the encounter could prove more enjoyable than he had anticipated.

Suddenly a large fat man was standing in the road waving a rolled-up newspaper.

Johnny stood on the brakes and cursed. He was about to remonstrate with the jay walker when he realised that it was a prospective fare anxious that the cab was not going to stop. He had been miles away.

## CHAPTER SIX

Johnny eased to a halt outside the neat florist shop at exactly 7 pm that evening. He was driving his own old Rover, a luxury he had considered selling on acquisition of the new black cab but he was glad now that he hadn't.

Claire must have been watching for him, as she appeared almost immediately on the doorstep, closing and double-locking the door carefully behind her. Smartly dressed in a neat blue woollen suit, which hugged her figure closely, and made-up with care, she looked most attractive.

Johnny took all this in at a glance and again had a twinge of conscience over the deception. This, however, was soon forgotten as she entered the car, saying cheekily

'Hello Johnny, I wondered if we would be travelling by cab?'

Johnny smiled. He, too, looked considerably smarter than the last time they had met and he answered flippantly 'No, I thought it would be more sociable if you sat beside me for a change - anyway I can't stand back seat drivers.'

She laughed lightly, tossing her head back in an attractive way. The movement sent an aroma of expensive perfume in Johnny's direction. He considered commenting on it but decided not to.

'Well I'm here - so where are you taking me?' she asked, turning to face Johnny.

'Actually, I've managed to get a couple of tickets for a jazz concert at the Fairfield Halls, if you're interested?'

'Umm, sounds good' she nodded with approval.

'And I thought we could grab a meal afterwards - you haven't eaten, have you?' he added anxiously.

'No, I haven't - and I'd like that very much.'

'Good, that's settled then' he said, and, putting the car into gear, drove southwards towards Croydon. It occurred to him that this was the second time he had made this journey in as many days, although this time it promised to be much more enjoyable.

They chatted amicably throughout the journey and soon Johnny was parking the car in the vast underground car park. Another reason why it was such a treat for him to come to Fairfield Halls or the Ashcroft Theatre was that there was always plenty of room to park. Even if the evening traffic approaching Croydon was heavy and the start of the show imminent, he could always find a space down below. This was the reverse of the situation when he attended a West End theatre, when the parking at that time of the evening would have been a nightmare.

'We've got time for a drink, if you fancy one' said Johnny, as they made their way up the wide marble stairway. 'I'd love one' replied Claire, looking up at Johnny with a smile. They threaded their way through the theatregoers into the bar and Johnny squeezed his way to the counter and before long re-appeared with two drinks. He was particularly pleased because he had managed to order the same for the interval, thus avoiding the usual struggle for service later. They sipped their drinks until the signal for the start of the performance sounded. Claire took Johnny's arm impulsively as they made their way to their seats in the centre of the stalls.

The concert was a huge success, as was the meal afterwards in the friendly Italian restaurant opposite, its walls covered with signed photographs of stars who had appeared at the Halls. An exceptionally good duo played and sang softly in the background as candles flickered on each table. The bottle of Chianti with the excellent meal had given both of them a feeling of well-being, as they relaxed with their liqueurs in the pleasant atmosphere.

Claire looked at the rugged, dark-haired man opposite and wondered just how long it would be before he, like the others, found out about her brothers and rapidly lost interest in her. Johnny, as if reading her thoughts, wondered how this woman, whose company he was enjoying so much, could possibly have come from the same parents as the evil brothers. He had started out with only one aim in view and that was to infiltrate the family, to find out as much as he could about them and then, by fair means or foul, to take revenge for his departed colleague. He certainly had not expected it to be easy and now, if his gut feeling proved correct, the task was likely to be even harder than anticipated.

They chatted and laughed noisily as the waiter kept them supplied with coffee, slowly finding out more about each other. Neither being completely truthful with the other.

Johnny though, had the advantage of knowing already about Claire's background, whereas she innocently believed everything he told her, since she had no reason to think otherwise. For his part, Johnny was working on the old adage that, for every lie told, two more would be needed to cover up and, therefore, he was keeping the deception to a minimum.

He was totally honest when explaining to her that he had been married, that it hadn't worked out and that he was now divorced. But when it came to filling in the past few years he simply extended his service in the Royal Marines and increased the length of time in the taxi business. In this way, he conveniently missed out the years of service in the police.

He called for the bill and soon they were being ushered out of the restaurant by the owner who, despite all his years in England, said goodnight in a heavy Italian accent. Retracing their steps to the underground car park, which was by now practically deserted, they were soon in the car and heading back to the little florist shop in Clapham.

When they pulled up outside, Johnny accepted Claire's offer to come up for a nightcap - after all, the reason for the evening out had been to acquaint himself with the layout of the shop and, as he now realised, the flat above it. After that he wasn't too sure what the next step would be.

Claire unlocked the shop door and, as they entered, they were greeted by the almost overpowering fragrance of what looked like hundreds of flowers, enclosed in the relatively small area. To Claire this was nothing unusual, she lived with it every day, but to Johnny the unexpected smell of the flowers added a pleasant touch to what had been a heart-searching evening for him. Claire snapped on a light, led the way across the room into a small passageway and started to climb the stairs to her flat.

Johnny looked quickly around him to memorise the layout, before climbing the stairs two-at-a-time to catch her up. At the rear of the shop, he had noticed a smaller room which obviously served as an office-cum-private room. The door was open and he could see a desk, a chair and a large green ex-government filing cabinet. 'Might be worth a look in there' he thought to himself. Outside this room, and leading off the passage, was a heavily-bolted door which obviously opened on to the mews behind the shop.

On the landing at the top of the stairs, Claire turned and entered a spacious lounge, switching on a couple of table lights as she did so. 'Make yourself comfortable' she called out over her shoulder, adding 'and what would you like to drink? I've got most things.'

'A small scotch on the rocks would be fine - shall I get it?'

'No, you sit there and relax' she insisted, busying herself with the glasses which she had produced from a drinks cabinet in one corner of the room. She moved through a doorway into a small kitchen to collect some ice and Johnny looked around the room. What he saw came as no surprise. Claire had imposed her personality on the room - it was neat, tidy and tastefully furnished.

She appeared with the drinks and handed Johnny his. She had poured herself a Campari and soda which she placed on a small table beside an armchair opposite him. Johnny noted this action particularly. There was plenty of room beside him on the settee and he thought to himself 'Well, at least she has made her intentions clear' as they raised their glasses and drank to a very pleasant evening.

They chatted until both drinks were finished and then, after a short interval, Claire announced 'Well Johnny, I'm going to throw you out now - some of us have to work in the morning, you know.'

'You're right there' replied Johnny 'I've got an early run to the airport so I'd better get some beauty sleep myself.'

As they both stood up, they were close, almost touching and Johnny reached out, placed a hand each side of her face, kissed her lightly on the cheek and then tenderly on the lips. He was aware that she moved closer to him and enjoyed the contact.

'Thanks for a most enjoyable evening' she said, looking fully into his eyes.

'It was good fun' replied Johnny 'we must do it again sometime.'

'I'd like that very much' said Claire, leading the way out of the room and down the stairs.

As he drove home, all kinds of thoughts went through his mind. He was pleased that he had achieved his aim, which was to get on the inside. As it turned out it had not been difficult, but he was uneasy over the fact that, despite the brief relationship, he really liked the girl. This was a situation that could only lead to complications later on, but it was a chance he would just have to take. Meanwhile, he had enjoyed the evening immensely and had the distinct feeling that, if the relationship continued to flourish, he would end up spending the night with her.

With this pleasant thought in mind, he entered his own cold, deserted flat.

******

Over the next few days, he escorted Claire to a variety of places from theatres to old Thames-side pubs, always avoiding places where he was likely to run into his old mates. The friendship developed until, as Johnny had anticipated, the evening arrived when she locked and bolted the front door of the little florist shop from the inside and, when they reached the flat upstairs, she gave him his scotch on the rocks. However, before his glass was empty, he had swept her up in his arms and carried her into the bedroom.

They made love tenderly, each enjoying the other's body as much as they had enjoyed each other's company since their first meeting. As they lay quietly together relaxing in each other's arms, Claire, unable to believe that the friendship could possibly last, felt certain that Johnny, like all the others, was bound to find out about her brothers, but she was determined to keep her fears a secret as long as possible.

Johnny's thoughts had also turned to the brothers, but in his case he was still unable to believe that this wonderful woman that he had just made love to, and whom he liked so much, could be related to those two. He had an even stranger feeling now that he would have to pay dearly at some time for the deception - but that was in the future. For the moment he felt happier than at any time since the early days of his marriage and he groaned loudly with pleasure as, instinctively, they reached for each other again. Afterwards, lying between that blissful state of exhilaration and exhaustion, Claire started jokingly to persuade Johnny to get up and make her a coffee. He was naturally reluctant to be parted from her and the warm bed for whatever reason. 'You promised me anything I desired just now' she chided. 'Yes, but I was lying' he joked, moving even closer to her.

Suddenly the illusion and the silence of the night was shattered by piercing sounds below outside the shop of screaming tyres, a roaring engine and the squealing of heavily-applied brakes. The hairs on the back of Johnny's neck stood up and his nerves jangled as his years of police training and experience alerted him to possible danger.

It certainly was not the sound of a car being driven normally. Almost at once his suspicions were confirmed, as he heard the sound of breaking glass, followed by the roaring of the same engine and gears responding to the urgent unreasonable demands of the driver. He leapt out of bed and crossed to the window just in time to see a large black car without lights disappearing rapidly into the distance.

Claire had screamed involuntarily at the sound of breaking glass and he came quickly back to comfort her. 'Put some clothes on quickly' he ordered, at the same time hastily pulling on his trousers and slipping into his shoes. He grabbed his shirt and disappeared through the doorway, clattering quickly down the stairs and into the passageway, with the sound of Claire's voice 'Johnny, be careful' in his ears.

He paused outside the door of the shop with his hand on the handle. His nostrils confirmed what he had most feared. It wasn't a brick that had come through the window - it was a Molotov cocktail, and the room was on fire. He quickly unlocked and unbolted the door leading to the mews at the rear.

'Get down here quickly, Claire' he yelled up the stairs. Almost immediately she appeared, white-faced and frightened, pulling on a dressing gown, unsure of what the danger was; a marked contrast to the girl who had looked so calm and contented in his arms a few minutes earlier. 'Quick, outside' he ordered, as she came racing down the stairs, the dressing gown streaming out behind her.

Near the bottom of the stairs, he grabbed her and, opening the back door, he pushed her roughly outside into the mews, shouting 'Ring the Fire Brigade.'

'What are you going to do?' she screamed anxiously.

'Never mind - do as I say quickly' he ordered, slamming the back door shut.

'What was he going to do?' Alone, his thoughts racing, he called on all his training and experience. He coughed loudly as smoke from the shop forced its way under the door into the passageway and entered his lungs. His eyes started to water. Thank God the inner shop door had been closed otherwise they could have been trapped upstairs.

He looked quickly into the doorway of the small back room which led off the passageway and there, in front of him, was the green ex-government filing cabinet which might contain details of the Steadman business. Something which he had intended somehow to inspect at the earliest opportunity.

He allowed himself a smile at the irony of the situation. Now that he had the opportunity, the bloody place was on fire. Seeing a fire extinguisher on the wall, he automatically lifted it down and left the room. The whole passageway was now filled with yellow, acrid smoke which tore at his lungs and attacked his eyes. The situation was pretty hopeless. As long as the shop door remained closed there was good chance that the fire would be confined to the shop itself, provided the Brigade arrived soon. Fortunately they were stationed locally, only a few streets away, so that shouldn't be too long. He decided that there was nothing to be gained by remaining on the premises so, opening the rear door slightly, he quickly slipped out into the mews, slamming the door behind him.

He gulped mouthfuls of fresh air into his lungs as he ran around to the front of the shop and was welcomed by the sounds of clanging bells in the distance.

An anxious Claire fell into his arms, gabbling 'Are you alright. One of the neighbours opposite called the Brigade almost as soon as it happened.'

'I'm alright, don't worry' he replied, his face blackened by the smoke and now streaked as tears made their way down his cheeks. 'Are the people next door out?'

'Yes, they're all out – I've spoken to them - they're all over there.'

She pointed to a group of people huddled together, waiting anxiously, on the other side of the road.

Other neighbours in immediate danger, who had vacated their houses clutching articles of value, stood in groups watching anxiously.

The fire, though blazing well, looked as if it was still being contained in the one room despite the spread of petrol. Smoke and sparks billowed out of the large shop window broken by the bomb and sounds could be heard of glass vases and containers exploding inside. Claire hung on tightly to Johnny as they stood helplessly watching, unable to do anything as the business that she and her father had worked so hard to build up disappeared before her eyes. The only consolation was that she and Johnny were both safe and well - it could have been so different.

Round the corner, with engines roaring and bells clanging, came the fire engines - two pumps, one in close pursuit of the other. They were so close to the Station that the fire crew were still getting dressed. They dealt proficiently with the fire, pouring gallons of water through the window and then, after breaking open the front door and taking the hoses through, they soon had the fire completely under control. In no time the shop was just smouldering, the entire room gutted but damage was confined to that room and had not affected the upstairs. Like the US Cavalry, the Brigade had arrived just in time.

The neighbours and sightseers made their way slowly back to their respective houses greatly relieved and, no doubt, exaggerated accounts of the fire would be related to friends and colleagues with great enthusiasm the following day.

The police had arrived almost as quickly as the fire brigade and had taken charge. Johnny had a few anxious moments, especially when called upon to make a brief statement. Fortunately, he wasn't known to the uniformed Duty Officer and the young constables who had attended; but as the bombing would become a CID matter it was only a matter of time before Claire would discover his true identity. For the moment though, his exertions before and after the fire had left him exhausted and he would deal with that problem when it arose.

They made their way back into the house from the rear. The smoke had cleared and apart from the horrible smell and discolouration of the ceiling at the top of the landing the rooms upstairs remained unaffected. Johnny sank gratefully on to the large settee, his eyes red-rimmed and his nose and mouth blackened by the smoke. He would have a bath later, but for the moment he just wanted to relax.

Claire crossed to the drinks table and poured two large scotches. Handing Johnny his, she sat down close to him, and said anxiously 'Johnny, I've been thinking. If the fire was started by a petrol bomb, who would do that to me and why? I've never upset anybody.'

Johnny avoided her glance. It was a question that he knew would be asked eventually. 'It's a mystery to me, but perhaps the police will be able to find out' he replied, at the same time wondering if the plan he had put into operation with his snout Smithy had started to work. If so - it had bloody nearly backfired.

## CHAPTER SEVEN

Bobby Steadman, Claire's father, yawned, scratched himself once more and downed his third cup of tea, despite the fact it was still only 4.30 am. He was one of those small wiry characters without an ounce of fat and as tough as old boots. He had worked hard all his life and couldn't break the habit. Having attained the age of 70 he knew that if he stopped it would be curtains.

Reaching for his old chequered cloth cap, he completed the uniform of the old-style stallholder with the cross-over neckerchief above his collarless shirt.

He always wore a neckerchief, even on Sunday with his best grey suit. They could change fashion as much as they like but Bobby Steadman wore the old traditional style and had no intention of changing for anyone.

He closed the front door of the neat family home on the Clapham Common borders, climbed into the old van parked in the street outside and headed towards Vauxhall and the New Covent Garden.

'Not a patch on the old one' he would often remark 'that place really had character.'

Like so many of his contemporaries who had attended the 'old Garden' for most of their lives - some going back to the days of the old horse and cart - Bobby missed the daily visit terribly.

'Anyway, it ain't the same since they tarted the place up and turned it into a load of poncy shops' he would grumble.

On rising, he had popped his head round the door of Claire's bedroom and the undisturbed bed made him smile, as he realised that she had spent the night at her own flat.

He smiled again, saying out loud 'I 'ope she enjoyed 'erself - she deserves it, that girl. I'll pull her leg when I see 'er at the shop.' The thought pleased him and he looked forward to seeing his daughter.

'The only good thing left in my life now' he would often say. He tolerated the brothers only because they were his own flesh and blood and he felt that some of the responsibility for them turning out the way they had must be down to him.

He was completely oblivious of the fire at the shop, which had occurred a few hours earlier, and had no way of knowing that the boxes of flowers he was about to buy at the market were for a shop that had been completely gutted. The van trundled along Clapham Commonside, turning left as he passed the boating pool, which was deserted except for a few ducks bobbing up and down like the float on the end of some fisherman's line.

Bobby Steadman was a real cockney. He loved his London, with all its complexities and contrasts. At the moment, the streets were fairly deserted except for those like him heading for the new Garden or others who had to cross London and were making the journey before the rush hour started. Lights were starting to appear in houses as Londoners prepared for work in the great Metropolis. He loved this time of the day almost as much as later, when London came alive with all the hustle and bustle - something he always enjoyed and was still proud to be a part of.

He glanced at his watch. He was early, as usual, and, as it was dry and sunny, he decided to make a detour and drive past his first house, down near the Battersea Dogs Home, where they had all lived in happier days, when the family were all young. Crossing over the Wandsworth Road and down the hill the old van rattled and shook.

'Should get a new one, I s'pose' he said to himself, and then changing his mind added 'Nah, this one'll see me out.'

The road flattened out and he approached a full left turn, part of the one way system which led to Queenstown Road. He changed down and eased his foot onto the brake pedal - nothing happened and his foot went right down to the floor.

'Christ' he shouted, stamping his foot several times on the brake pedal without response. His heart rate increased alarmingly as he realised that he had no brakes. He grabbed the handbrake and jerked it back hard; although it seemed to take up at first, the handle then flew back loose in his hand. The van shook even more and the rear doors, like those in all old vans, fought each other noisily as the speed increased, almost out of control. He wrestled with the wheel hoping to steer the van to safety; he was tough and strong for his age but the situation rapidly became too much for him to handle.

Sweat broke out on his old, lined forehead and his eyes darted wildly from side to side in a panic as he tried to think of what to do next. In desperation he tried to crash the gear lever into a lower gear but this produced only a scream of protest from the gearbox, as the cogs tried to enmesh and were rejected. The gear lever kicked violently in his hand, sending a bolt of pain through his wrist and up his arm. With a yell and a curse he let go, grabbing the steering wheel again. Now in neutral and rapidly gaining speed, the van crashed headlong into a series of iron bollards put there just for the purpose of preventing vehicles from entering a paved, tree-filled area in front of some terraced houses.

Bob had only time to think 'Christ, no seat belt. Claire'll kill me' before his ears filled with the sound of tearing metal and the windscreen shattering, as he was thrown headlong through it and landed with a sickening thud into the base of one of the trees. The van keeled over with a slow deliberate movement, almost like a slow-motion replay, and settled with a loud crash, showering bits of metal, glass and dried mud all over the scene. The dust then settled and there was silence, the only movement coming from the two wheels that faced the sky and which spun noiselessly round and round until they too stopped.

Suddenly a front door burst open and a large fat man appeared from one of the houses with his hair dishevelled, still adjusting a pair of hastily pulled-on trousers and trying at the same time to tuck in the tail of a vest. He was joined quickly by another early riser who, as the particles of white foam on his face indicated, had been in the act of shaving when the accident occurred.

'My missus is calling the ambulance' he blurted out, as the two men met beside the motionless figure of Bob Steadman, whose old lined face, lacerated by the windscreen, was covered in blood.

'Don't think it'll do much good' panted the fat man, who was almost out of breath with his exertions. 'Looks as if the tree finished him off, poor sod.'

'Not a lot we can do, then' agreed the smaller man 'just wait for the law I s'pose.'

They hadn't long to wait as a police area car, with a crew of three, arrived first in response to the telephone call. They were closely followed by the local Duty Officer, a young Inspector, who immediately assumed control. A quick check confirmed that Bobby Steadman was no longer 'of this world'. His neck had snapped on impact with the tree - ironic, really, because he loved flowers and trees.

'Guvnor. Take a look at this' piped up one sharp-eyed member of the area car crew, who was checking the van over. The Inspector left the crumpled body and joined the PC, who was bent double examining the dirty underside of the van.

'There Guvnor, look' he said proudly, pointing to the brake pipes and the cables of the hand brake. They had been crudely hacksawed half through.

Through his quick actions, Johnny Spencer had been able to save the daughter of the Steadman family but unfortunately there had been no one around to do the same for the father.

# CHAPTER EIGHT

Sunlight streamed through the window of Claire's flat. The street outside was noisy with people and traffic as Londoners made their way to work.

Johnny awoke with a start from a deep sleep, wondering where the hell he was. His eyes, red-rimmed and bloodshot from the effects of the smoke, stung intensely and watered freely as he blinked to try to clear them. His mouth and lips were dry and tasted of a mixture of smoke and whisky. A coloured blanket covered him as he lay stretched out on the large settee, still wearing the clothes he had hastily pulled on the night before. As he came to, slowly the events of the previous night flooded back to him. First the evening at the theatre with Claire, followed by their lovemaking for the first time. He smiled and took some comfort from the pleasure it had given them both - only to be spoilt by the bloody petrol bomb and the fire. 'Who the hell had thrown the bomb?' he wondered 'and why?'

He had crashed out after drinking a large scotch handed to him by Claire. Claire! 'Where was she?' he looked around anxiously. Suddenly he heard a commotion, the noise of which must have awakened him. He could hear loud voices, then Claire's, slightly hysterical above the others, followed by the sounds of footsteps ascending the stairs. He sat up quickly and, anticipating trouble, threw off the blanket and swung his legs round to the floor, despite the fact that he was still half asleep.

'I must be going mad' he thought 'I'm still keyed up after last night.'

His instincts proved correct - he had reason to be keyed up, for into the room burst Claire, white-faced and trembling, followed by two men. Johnny's heart thumped hard inside his chest as he recognised the Steadman brothers immediately. Directly behind Claire stood Vic, slightly-built and looking ten years older than the last time they had met across a court room at the Old Bailey. His face had that sickly pallor that only years in prison can produce. His eyes, though, were black and piercing and they searched the room anxiously, giving the impression that at least his mental alertness was unaffected. Vic had always been the brains of the two and the evil one.

Just a pace behind Vic, as usual, was Billy, his huge frame filling the doorway.

Physically he looked even bigger than the last time they had met and looked as if he had weathered the years inside much better than his brother. One thing that had not changed, though, was the expression on his face; a slightly bewildered look as if someone had just punched him straight between the eyes.

Both pairs of eyes bore into him in disbelief and Johnny felt a wave of fear pass through him. He shivered involuntarily and his sleep-befuddled brain tried desperately to function, without much success. He was trapped - there was nowhere to go.

'So this is the marvellous bloke who just happened to be around to save you from the fire' Vic Steadman spat the words out contemptuously, his lips curling in disgust.

'You stupid bitch' he continued 'don't you know who this bastard is?'

Claire, wide-eyed and confused, stared at Johnny but replied defiantly 'He's called Johnny - Johnny Spencer.'

'Yes, Johnny ex-bloody Detective bloody Sergeant Spencer. He's the guy who put us away. What the fuckin' hell's he doing here?' In a rage, his left hand swept out viciously and caught Claire on the nose and mouth, sending her reeling across the room, blood spilling from her nose.

Johnny automatically jumped to his feet and Vic moved quickly to one side as Billy, with a move that belied his bulk, crashed on top of Johnny, pinning him back down on the settee. It was a well-rehearsed move, one which had been put into operation many times when Billy's brawn was required. In a flash Vic was beside Johnny's head and the tip of an evil-looking knife touched Johnny's throat just deep enough to draw blood.

'Go on, struggle you bastard' he hissed 'Give me more reason than I've got already to stick you.'

The cold, menacing words delivered in a flat monotone, together with the feeling of warm blood running down his neck, not to mention the huge panting mass of Billy Steadman on top of him were enough to make Johnny give in, beaten for the moment.

Billy, who was always short on words - and brains - panted 'Stick the bastard, Vic, he's asked for it.'

'Not yet, Billy Boy' replied Vic, with authority 'We've got to find out what he's doing here with her.' He jerked his head in the direction of Claire and added, menacingly, 'Don't worry, you'll get your chance Billy. But not here. Is there a basement under the shop, stupid sister?' he hurled the words at Claire.

'Find out for your bloody self' blazed Claire defiantly from the corner where she had landed. Blood still poured from her nose as a result of the blow from her older brother.

'Just you stay here, stupid. I've got words to say to you later.' He had withdrawn the knife from Johnny's throat and pointing it now in his sister's direction emphasised each word with it. Turning his attention back to Johnny he said 'Find something to truss him up with Billy. I don't want to take any chances with this clever bastard – he's got a reputation for being a bit useful.' He returned the knife point to Johnny's throat.

Billy eased himself off and grinned 'Be a pleasure, Vic. I never thought I'd be back in action so quick after being inside.' He strode towards the kitchen and sounds could be heard as Billy pulled out drawers and generally threw things around during his search. Eventually he reappeared triumphantly waving a nylon indoor clothes line and, turning Johnny over, they tied his hands behind his back, tightening the cord until it cut savagely into his wrists. The long end of the cord was pulled upwards, wrapped twice around his throat and finally around Billy's huge fist. With glee he jerked Johnny on to his feet saying 'Lead on, Vic - one false move and I'll cut his fuckin' 'ead off.'

Johnny stumbled forward and, trussed as he was with the cord cutting into his throat, he had no option but to do as he was told. Before leaving the room he had time only to cast a concerned glance in Claire's direction. She was still lying dazed in one corner and his eyes were met by a mixture of bewilderment and disbelief, as tears ran down her tortured face and mingled with the blood still issuing from her nose. He was driven down the stairs, with Billy laughingly jerking the cord tight at the slightest excuse and into the small passageway at the bottom where Vic soon found what he was looking for.

There was a door under the stairs. The switch just inside the door produced enough light from a single dusty and cobweb-covered bulb to reveal a short flight of narrow wooden stairs leading into a large basement room. It was filled with an assortment of junk accumulated over the years including dozens of empty and dusty flat wooden flower boxes, relics of the days before lighter, more modern packaging systems.

Like most old basements which were covered in dirt and cobwebs, it was damp and smelt of ageing walls and crumbling mortar, not to mention rotting vegetation which, in turn, had attracted mice. Some of these, protesting at the unwelcome intrusion into their dark quiet world, squeaked and scuttled for cover as the procession made its way noisily down the old wooden stairs. The floor was still wet with the water used to put out the fire in the room above.

Johnny's face had turned crimson, his eyes bulged and the veins on his neck stood out like knotted rope as he gasped for breath. He tried desperately to force his brain to function above the pain. 'How the hell was he going to extricate himself from this situation?' He had been in a few tight spots before now whilst serving with the Marines in Northern Ireland, not to mention those times when he was working for the Squad out of the Yard. The difference then was the tremendous back-up which had always been readily available at the end of a personal radio. Alone now, he couldn't remember ever feeling so vulnerable, so utterly helpless. Warm blood pumped from his neck as pressure forced it from the wound made by the knife.

On reaching the bottom step, Billy, with a playful almost childish laugh, tripped his prisoner, releasing the cord just in time to prevent decapitating Johnny, who crashed to the floor. 'Steady Billy' rasped Vic, his eyes narrowing 'I want the bastard to be able to talk' adding 'Don't worry, you'll get your fun later, like I promised.'

The basement contained three six-inch metal poles fixed to the floor and bolted on to a huge metal beam which provided added support for the floor above. Billy dragged Johnny to one of these, jerked him to his feet, undid the cord around his neck and secured his hands to the pole behind his back. Johnny gasped for air, thankful that the cord was no longer choking him, but only too aware of the vulnerable position that he was now in. He breathed deeply and braced himself for what he knew was sure to follow.

The brothers stood in front of him grinning in anticipation. He could smell them.

Their clothes reeked of prison. A mixture of disinfectant and human bodies. At an almost indiscernable nod from Vic, Billy crashed his right fist into Johnny's solar plexis, causing him to cry out as the breath was expelled from his body. He felt a wave of nausea pass over him as he struggled to remain conscious, the cord cutting deeply into his wrists as the weight of his body jerked forward.

'Now you bastard, I want to know and I want to know quickly. What are you doing here with my sister.' Vic spat the words out.

'Pure coincidence' mumbled Johnny, and he lied as he added 'I didn't even know she was your sister.'

'You lying bastard pig' screamed Vic, as he nodded again to Billy who repeated the blow only, this time, slightly higher and to the right. The pain was excruciating and Johnny screamed as he felt the bottom of his rib cage snap.

'I'm not a lawman anymore, you must know that' he coughed defiantly, each word an effort to produce. They must know that he was no longer in the Force - the prison underground information system would have kept them informed of this.

'Oh, I know that alright, pig - but you, my stupid sister, and a petrol bomb all at the same time has got to be too much of a coincidence.'

'Let me 'ave a go on the other side, Vic' beamed Billy, warming to his task.

'No, hold it - this bastard's not stupid and I want him to be able to talk.'

'He's not stupid' agreed Billy 'but he's a greedy bastard. Don't forget, Vic, he had the money and still put us away. We bloody well owe him some stick.'

Johnny through the pain, thought to himself 'I'd better start talking' and grunted 'What do you mean? You tried to stitch us up. We never had any money - you bloody well know that.'

Billy drew his huge fist back again but Vic restrained him, insisting 'Don't give us that shit, Spencer - your mate had the money alright, all £10,000 of it and you must have got your share.'

'I don't believe it' insisted Johnny 'Albert was as straight a copper as you're likely to find.'

'That doesn't say much' interrupted Billy contemptuously 'You're all on the bloody take.'

'But we heard he'd snuffed it' grinned Vic 'and serve the bastard right. Anyway he won't fit anyone else up.'

Johnny was puzzled 'Why should these two insist, in this way and after all this time, that Albert had taken a bribe? It was all water under the bridge as far as he was concerned - unless? No, it wasn't possible. Albert was as straight as a die and he had worked with him long enough to know. There had been many opportunities for them to have made a fortune, but they hadn't. So why were these two bastards insisting that they had taken the bribe money? It didn't make sense. They must have got their wires crossed somewhere.'

He was jerked out of his thoughts by a vicious backhander across his face from Vic, who usually left the physical stuff to his brother. He was clearly starting to lose his patience.

'What about the petrol bomb then, pig? How do you explain that?' he screamed, through clenched teeth and with his black eyes piercing Johnny's pain-racked brain. He felt warm blood oozing from his nose and also from his cheek where a large ring on Vic's finger had split his skin. His brain was working overtime. 'I've got to give them something concrete, otherwise I'm going to end up a wreck.'

'You're a thick pair of buggers, aren't you? Christ it doesn't take much to work out that someone isn't too pleased to see you two coming out of the nick. Someone's not keen to see you back on the scene again.'

'Like who?' questioned Billy.

'Christ, I don't know' snapped Johnny impatiently 'but it wouldn't be too hard to find out.' Then, glaring at Vic, he taunted 'You're the one who boasts that you keep tabs on everything that's going on outside while you're still in the nick.' He paused, as he could see that he had Vic thinking. 'You must know who's been running things' he added slowly.

'He could be right, Vic' burst out Billy, enthusiastically.

'Shut up' snarled his brother 'I don't trust this bastard, but it's possible. There must be one or two I can think of who won't be pleased to see us back.' He paused, his brain searching for a possible answer. Billy kept quiet - the thinking was always done by his brother. Vic started to speak, softly and slowly at first 'But - it doesn't explain - how he comes to be with Claire' he exploded, lashing across Johnny's face again as he reached his sister's name.

Johnny's head jerked back and then dropped forward onto his chest, blood dripping from a fresh wound. His head was splitting, he was sure that one of his ribs was broken, and the pain was intense. Vic shook the hand he had just used on Johnny's face and blood spattered on to the dusty floor. He examined the hand closely. The ring which had split Johnny's face had dug into the underside of his own finger, cutting it to the bone, and blood was pouring from it. The sight didn't please him. He wasn't too fussy about other people's blood but this was his own and he cursed himself for not leaving the rough stuff to Billy. He automatically took his finger to his mouth to ease the pain and stem the flow. His piercing eyes bore deep into Johnny's, his feelings of hatred rising to the surface once more, and Johnny braced himself.

Billy, seeing his brother in pain, pleaded 'Come on, Vic, just give me five minutes with him and I promise he'll talk.' He, too, was getting angry, after all this was his speciality and his brother usually left all that to him. Vic was supposed to be the brains and now he'd got himself injured and, in his simple way, he thought to himself 'Serve him right, he should have left it to me.' After all, hadn't he used his years inside to improve himself physically? Every opportunity had been taken to work out and, what with weight training and circuit training, he had never been in better shape and was dying to use up some of the excess power which was bursting within him and, now, in defiance of his brother, he stepped forward towards Johnny, but Vic stepped between them, recognising the signs. He had found it necessary, on several occasions, to pull Billy off some poor victim to prevent a possible manslaughter charge.

'No, wait Billy' he persuaded 'this bastard needs more subtle treatment.' His eyes narrowed and he smiled at the prospect of what he had in mind.

'Like what?' snarled Billy, still not happy with the way things were going.

'Like maybe using Spike Johnson's speciality.' Vic paused and looked straight into his brother's eyes, waiting for the penny to drop. Slowly Billy's brain accepted the idea and his face broke into a smile. 'Yeah, yeah, that's a great idea, Vic.' He stepped back and relaxed.

'Think you can fix it up, Billy?' asked Vic, spitting blood from his mouth and grinning, his teeth still red with the blood from his finger.

'No problem' replied Billy enthusiastically 'there must be some wire upstairs.'

'Come on then, I could do with a break.' Vic shook the blood from his hand again, saying 'This bastard's not going anywhere the way you've tied him up.' They turned and made their way back up the stairs, their footsteps echoing at first and then becoming faint as they reached the flat.

Alone in the cellar, Johnny eased the cord from side to side around the pole and pressed downwards. Each movement sent a stabbing pain through his left side where he feared the rib was broken. Finally, with sweat pouring from him, he was able to sit on the floor and take some of the weight off his wrists. Exhausted, he would have loved to relax for a while, but all his instincts for self-preservation flooded to him, all his background in the

Marines and the police screamed to him to 'Think! Think!' of a way to get free before the brothers returned.

His eyes searched around him desperately. The only thing within reach was one of the stacks of old wooden flower crates and he could see that they had been strengthened around with thin wire. 'Maybe! Just maybe!' if he could find a sharp end he might be able to sever the nylon cord. It was worth a try. Stretching out as far as he could, his ribs screaming in protest, he managed to get one foot around the bottom of the stack.

'I'm going to have to pull them down on top of me and it's bound to make a hell of a noise' he mumbled to himself 'still there's nothing else for it.' With a jerk, he pulled the stack towards him. He twisted his head sideways to avoid one crate which caught him a violent blow on the shoulder, as the stack of crates crashed around him. The noise was deafening. 'They must have heard it' he thought. As he held his breath, not only to listen for returning footsteps but also to avoid breathing in the dust and debris of years which had been disturbed, he examined the crates and, sure enough, one of them had a sharp end of wire sticking out - and it was within reach. He wriggled into position and, after several attempts, managed to start picking the nylon cord on to the wire end. The sweat poured into his eyes from his efforts but he could not tell if any progress was being made behind him. All he knew was that each pick at the wire sent fresh surges of pain through his arms to his brain. Time was running out - they must return soon.

He stabbed harder at the wire, trying to blot out the pain. Almost exhausted with his efforts, he slumped back against the pole, his ears alert. 'Shit, they're coming back!' He could hear footsteps descending the stairs and he quickly changed his position, hoping against hope that they would not realise what he had been up to.

Vic was leading and Billy, grinning from ear to ear, was close behind carrying a quantity of electrical flex which looked as if it had belonged to the table lamp upstairs.

Johnny's heart sank and he thought 'Oh Christ! That's what they meant by Spike Johnson's speciality.'

Vic spoke first 'I told you this bastard's not to be trusted. He's pulled these crates down.' He viciously kicked one of them out of the way and then he kicked out again, his shoe digging into Johnny's kidney region as he lay helpless on the floor.

'Hurry up, Billy, get it fixed up.' Billy looked around the basement. 'There's nowhere to plug it in' he whined helplessly.

'Oh, for Christ's sake, there's one over there above the bench' snapped Vic impatiently. 'Oh, yeah, good idea, Vic' nodded Billy as he went across and plugged the flex in. Meanwhile, Vic reached around Johnny from behind the pole, undid the buckle of his belt and pulled it through.

Then, chuckling at the prospect of what was about to happen, he undid the hook on Johnny's trousers and zipped the fly down.

Johnny, who was in no doubt now about what was to happen, struggled as best he could but to no avail. He was completely vulnerable - and he knew it. Suddenly, without warning, his own belt was around his throat and his head cracked backwards against the metal pole. With a horrible laugh, Vic started to turn the belt like a tourniquet. 'You're going to talk, you bastard Spencer. Sooner or later, it doesn't matter, but you're going to talk.'

As the strap cut deeper into his throat, Johnny fought for breath. His face reddened, the veins stuck out in his throat, and his eyeballs felt as it they were about to leave their sockets.

'Talk! Talk! Talk!' persisted Vic, emphasising each word with a jerk on the belt. In his already weakened condition, Johnny's brain, starved of oxygen, finally succumbed and his head dropped onto his chest. His system had taken all that it could for the moment and he had passed out.

Vic immediately loosened the belt and, coming round to face him suspiciously, kicked him again, saying 'Come on, you bastard, is this another of your tricks?' It dawned on him slowly, after a few more kicks, that Johnny was indeed unconscious. 'Billy' he yelled 'get a bucket of water down here quick.'

The sounds of Billy crossing the floor above and a tap being turned on could be heard, and soon he appeared in the doorway carrying a large metal flower vase that had survived the fire, full of water. Seeing Johnny slumped and lifeless, he complained bitterly 'Christ, what have you done, Vic? You wouldn't let me touch him - is he a goner?'

'No. you daft bastard, give me the water' and, spilling some of the water as he snatched the vase, he dashed the remainder into Johnny's face.

Suddenly, at the noise of the cellar door opening, both men spun round anxiously.

It was Claire, white-faced and trembling. She cried out, involuntarily, as she looked past her brothers and saw the slumped figure of Johnny, his face split and covered in blood.

'What do you want, stupid?' sneered Vic 'come to see your boy friend?'

'No' she gasped 'it's Dad.'

'What about Dad?' said Billy.

'He's been in an accident at the bottom of Silverthorne Road and they've taken him to hospital.' She paused for breath and continued 'One of his mates on his way back from the market saw the van crashed over and the ambulance leaving.' The words came tumbling out and, feeling faint, she hung onto the stair banister.

'You fit enough to drive?' demanded Vic curtly.

'Yes' whispered Claire 'I'll be alright.'

'Right - they must have taken him to Battersea General. Come on, it'll only take a few minutes.'

'What about him?' said Billy, nodding towards the lifeless figure of Johnny.

'He'll keep - the bastard's not going anywhere. He's got a lot of talking to do yet.' Claire led the way back upstairs and soon they were in her car heading for the hospital.

# CHAPTER NINE

The previous hour had been sheer agony for Claire. What she dreaded most had happened and sooner than expected. She always knew that one day her brothers would be released from prison and that one of the happiest stages of her life would end. She had been free to lead her own life and at the same time look after her ageing father. Now he had been taken to hospital. 'Please God he's not badly hurt.' she murmured. Perhaps now she would be able to persuade her father to go away with her – anywhere, even to emigrate - anything to make a new life away from her brothers.

She drew some comfort from the thought of the contingency plans she had made; the two sets of accounts and her private bank account. Thank God she had been sensible enough to make these preparations well in advance.

When Vic had smashed her to the floor earlier she had lain there for several minutes in a daze, her head spinning. She could feel blood running from her nose and had automatically raised her hand to check it. Taking it away again as she struggled to focus her eyes, she saw that it was covered in blood and the sight of it jolted her back to her senses. She tried to stand up but fell back against the wall. Feeling her way along the wall, she staggered to the bathroom, ran the cold water tap and splashed several handfuls of water on to her aching face. Pinching her nose to stop the flow of blood, she looked at herself in the mirror. 'God, I look a mess' she thought. Her nose and top lip were beginning to swell and her teeth on one side ached. She touched them, gingerly, in turn and sighed with relief, satisfied that they were not loose.

'With a bit of luck I might get away with just a couple of black eyes and some swelling' she murmured, moving her face closer to the mirror. 'That bastard Vic will pay for this, somehow or other' she promised herself. Suddenly a cold feeling enveloped her body and she started to shake, the events of the previous evening, the fire followed by the appearance of her brothers and the violence to Johnny, had been too much for her system. As quickly as her weakening legs could take her, she weaved her way back to the lounge and grabbed the brandy bottle and a glass, the one rattling against the other as she poured the yellow liquid quickly into the glass. Raising it shakily, she closed her eyes tightly and gulped the liquor down her throat and into her body. A few seconds later it seemed to explode within and sent a warm pleasant feeling throughout her. She collapsed on to the settee and closed her eyes.

'What can I do?' she wondered, taking a smaller drink and desperately fighting to regain her composure. All she could see in front of her was the image of Johnny being led out of the room, his hands tied behind him and the end of the nylon cord around his neck being held by that madman Billy. Was he really an ex-Detective Sergeant? They certainly recognised him immediately and were certain that he was the one who had put them in prison. If so, was it just coincidence that they had met? 'Please God let it be so' she said out loud.

'It could be he was a cabby now' she argued to herself. 'Was it by design that he had entered her little shop to buy flowers?'

She remembered how she had dropped the bunch she was holding and how both of them had scrambled around on the floor picking them up. Since that day she had enjoyed his company more than anyone who had gone before. He had to be genuine.

'But what about the petrol bomb?' The brothers had accused him of having something to do with that. But hadn't he been marvellous and, maybe, saved her life during the fire? And now he was downstairs at the mercy of those animals. 'What were they doing to him?' she gulped again, and as she emptied the glass her heart jumped at the sound of footsteps coming back up the stairs.

Billy was the first to enter and, seeing Claire on the sofa with a glass in her hand, he remarked 'Here, Vic, she's boozin' now.'

'Never mind about that, have you got any spare light flex in the flat?'

'No – no' replied Claire 'what do you want it for?'

'Just a little something for your friend' grinned Billy 'I'm sure he'll like it.'

'This'll do' said Vic, picking up a small table lamp off a nest of tables in one corner of the room. He bent down, unplugged it from the socket and with a swift movement jerked the wires free from the lamp end.

Claire, angry at seeing her lamp treated in this way, opened her mouth to protest but before any sound could come out Vic pointed at her saying 'And you can shut your mouth, sister, 'cos you are the cause of all this bother.'

Seeing the empty glass in her hand he ordered 'You might as well make yourself bloody useful and pour Billy and me a drink - whisky.' Claire's first reaction was to refuse but, realising that it would probably only lead to another backhander, she rose and crossed to the drinks table. Pouring out a whisky for each of them, she handed one to Vic who looked at her contemptuously, saying 'That's better, now you are being a sensible girl.' Billy, grinning stupidly, reached out and accepted his drink, the whisky glass appearing minute in his giant-sized hand. 'Their latest spell in prison hasn't changed either of them' thought Claire 'Vic's just as evil and Billy's just as stupid.'

They both downed their drink in one go, Billy remarking 'At least she's got some decent booze, Vic.'

'Yeah, but that's all she's got - come on' replied Vic, and armed with the flex they headed downstairs again.

'What are they going to do with that flex?' wondered Claire, as she racked her brains to think what to do next. 'Who could help her? Her father – that's it, she'd contact him – he'd know.' Almost as if by magic, the phone rang, shrilly, making her start. It was Joey Roberts, one of her father's old mates with the news about the accident.

\*\*\*\*\*\*

Claire pulled in through the hospital gates, parked the car, and all three of them made their way to reception. A call to casualty confirmed that a Mr. Robert Steadman had been admitted and the young Indian receptionist's eyes had looked sad as she directed them to report to the Sister in charge of casualty. They made their way swiftly along the vast corridors, the only sound being their footsteps echoing on the hard stone floor. Claire's making a staccato sound, Vic's lighter and quieter and finally Billy's, solid and heavy.

'How is he?' asked Claire anxiously, as the Sister approached them, obviously alerted by the call from reception.

'Doctor will tell you everything' she replied briskly 'If you will just come with me' and she led the way into a nearby office, where a white-coated middle-aged doctor sat behind a desk talking to a grey, balding police sergeant and a young constable. The sergeant seemed to be noting down something said by the doctor. The sight of them caused Vic and Billy to check visibly and Vic automatically closed the hand which had been streaming blood earlier and which was now covered with a huge plaster. It still hurt like hell but, knowing the way he had received the injury, the sight of the uniforms caused his heart to thump.

'Christ' he thought 'I never expected to be faced with the Law as quickly as this.' The Sister introduced them and left. Before the doctor could speak, Claire asked softly 'What has happened to my father? How bad is he?'

'Sit down please, Miss Steadman' replied the doctor, indicating a chair. The two police officers stood up and offered their seats to the brothers who, appreciating the irony of the situation, sat down, with a smile passing between them.

'Miss Steadman' said the doctor, in a voice that was kindly but at the same time very serious. 'Your father was involved in an accident.'

'Yes - yes, I know that, but where is he?' blurted out Claire anxiously, feeling that something was wrong.

'I'm afraid the accident was a fatal one, Miss Steadman. I'm very sorry.'

'Oh no – no' screamed Claire hysterically 'he's the only one I've got. It can't be.'

The doctor came quickly round to the front of the desk to console her, as by this time she was in a half-faint, sobbing desperately and almost completely out of control. The events of the past hours had caught up with her again. The brothers, uncomfortable at the sight of their sister so near to collapse and uncomfortable in the presence of the police, sat motionless as the news sank in. There had been no love lost between them and their father and, ever since they had been old enough to stand on their own feet, they had treated him with contempt.

'Give me a hand, Sergeant, will you' said the doctor, noting that neither brother had made any attempt to calm their sister. Together they half-carried Claire to a nearby small, examination room with a couch and made her comfortable. A few minutes later the doctor returned to the room.

In his absence, the two brothers sat tight-lipped, their usual manner in the presence of the police, but eventually the sergeant had spoken to Vic. 'Mr. Steadman, I would like to have a word with you about the accident. It appears that the brakes on your father's van had been tampered with. The CID will want to speak to you later about it.' Before Vic had a chance to reply, the doctor interrupted 'And there are certain formalities to be carried out here concerning your father. We've given your sister a sedative to quieten her down and she's resting, so if we can deal with our formalities first, then you'll be free for the police.'

'Yeah, sure, let's get on with it' replied Vic, not at all pleased. Too many things were happening over which he had no control - not a situation he liked to find himself in. First the fire and now his father dead, and something wrong with the brakes. It didn't make sense. His natural instincts told him that events were being orchestrated. 'That bastard Spencer has something to do with it, I'm sure' and he smiled to himself at the thought of the pleasure they would have getting it out of him.

Claire stopped sobbing and gradually quietened down as the sedative relaxed her; she felt herself drifting off to sleep. The young nurse attending to her drew the curtains and crept quietly out of the room leaving her to rest.

As she felt consciousness slipping away somehow she thought of Johnny. The news of her father had blocked him completely from her mind. She sat up quickly, shook her head and forced herself to wake up.

'Johnny' she cried. Her brothers had said that he was connected with the fire but she didn't believe them. Now her father was dead. 'Could Johnny have had something to do with that? No, it wasn't possible!' She shook her head again and swung her legs over the side of the couch and sat up.

'Even if he has got something to do with this, I can't allow those animals to torture him.'

She stood up unsteadily. Her head was thumping, as if it would explode. Slipping on her shoes and jacket, she crossed the room and slowly opened the door. The corridor was bustling, but there was no sign of the doctor or nurse who had dealt with her. She slipped out quickly, closed the door behind her and made her way as confidently as possible to the Reception. Smiling at the girl behind the desk, she persuaded her to call a cab, which arrived within minutes. Giving the cabby her home address she told him to 'step on it.'

In no time they were outside the shop. 'Wait for me, will you? I'll only be a minute' she said, dashing into the mews in order to enter by the back door. Her heart thumped as she opened the door and the smell of the fire immediately filled her nostrils.

Making her way as quickly as possible down the stairs to the cellar, she dreaded what she might find.

\*\*\*\*\*\*

Johnny was conscious now and apprehensive. He had heard the cab door slam and, when the mews door above him opened, his heart sank. They were back - he did not know how much longer he could hold out. Then he heard the clattering of footsteps on the stairs, which even in his confused state, he knew were not the footsteps of the Steadman brothers. He turned his head to see that it was Claire.

'Thank God it's you' he cried out, overjoyed at seeing her.

'Oh Johnny, what have they done to you?' she whispered, feeling sick at the sight of his swollen and blood-stained face, which was racked with pain. She sank down beside him, held him gently and kissed his parched lips with tears streaming down her face. Johnny could taste the salt from her tears as he kissed her back. Then Claire, realising that he could not hold her because his hands were tied behind him around the pole, cried 'Wait, Johnny, wait' and, rummaging in her handbag, produced a pair of sharp nail scissors. Moving round to the back of him, she cried out again, 'Oh Johnny, those bastards. I could kill them.' The tears streamed down her face when she saw his crimson, swollen and blood-covered wrists with the cord hardly visible where it had cut deeply. As gently as possible, she freed his hands. Slowly, he brought his arms round to the front and rested them on his thighs. The blood rushed through his freed wrists again, making them feel as if they were on fire. He shook his head fiercely to block out the pain. 'Never mind' he thought 'They'll heal. I'm alive and free.' All his natural instincts for survival surfaced. 'Must get out - must get away' hammered through his brain.

Claire helped him to his feet and he leant thankfully against the metal pole for support. The pole that had kept him prisoner now acted as a welcome crutch. His head was spinning, the pain from his wrists intense and he felt he was about to pass out again.

Claire supported him, saying 'Hang on, Johnny, hang on! Can you make it up the stairs?'

'Give me a hand and I'll make it alright' he said with determination. Slowly and painfully they reached the top of the stairs and paused in the passageway where only a few hours ago, he had stood deciding what action to take about the fire. The stench of smoke still hung in the air.

Claire opened the door to the mews and no time they were outside. She slammed the door, leaving it unlocked.

Johnny leant against the wall for support, gulping fresh air into his lungs - he felt better already - he was free.

'I've got to leave you' said Claire 'Will you be alright?'

'Yes, but where are you going?' he asked anxiously, noticing for the first time just how dreadful she looked, her nose and face swollen and red. He had been concerned only with his own welfare up until now.

'I can't explain, but trust me. I have to get back.' She kissed him quickly and was gone.

'Claire! Claire!' he cried out after her as she disappeared round the corner. 'What did she mean? Where did she have to get back to?'

Before he could move, he heard a taxi door slam and the cab drive rapidly away.

## CHAPTER TEN

Johnny stood in the mews, blinked his burning eyes and shook his head in an attempt to clear his tired brain - without much success - in fact, all that it did was to increase his splitting headache.

He had to think and work out his next move. Claire had obviously tricked her brothers somehow in order to return and free him. 'What a girl – she's certainly got guts. Whatever happens, I'll repay her' he promised himself.

The thought of the brothers was enough to make Johnny realise that his most pressing concern at the moment was to put as much distance between himself and them as possible. He could just imagine how angry they would be on their return to find that he had escaped. He dug a hand deep into his trousers' pocket - even this action caused considerable pain, his head swam again and he clung to the wall for support. 'Good, the car keys are still there and the car should be parked where I left it.'

He pushed himself off the wall and staggered out of the mews, his head down, acutely aware of the picture he must present to anyone passing. Reaching the car, he opened the driver's door and collapsed, thankfully, into the seat. The familiar feel of the comfortable seat of the Rover was more than welcome.

He started the engine, painfully shifted the gear lever into first and pulled away.

Gaining speed as he passed the burnt-out shop, he could hardly believe that only twelve hours had passed since he had stayed the night there with Claire. So much had happened since then. First, the petrol bomb, then the fire, then the untimely release of the brothers from prison, followed by his capture and torture. And finally Claire, looking dreadful, had freed him but then she 'had to get back? Get back to where?' Her brothers were obviously still in control of her. He had an uneasy gut feeling that the trouble he had cooked up with Smithy was only just beginning.

He headed west, each gear change tearing at his ribs, until he settled for second gear - much to the annoyance of other drivers who thought he was mad sticking to the 30 mph speed limit. They showed their annoyance as only impatient London drivers can, by hooting and overtaking aggressively. Glaring angrily at Johnny, they quickly changed their tune on seeing the cut, smoke-blackened and blood-streaked face with bloodshot eyes staring back at them. They were only too glad to drive away as quickly as possible - it looked like trouble and nobody ever wanted to get involved in trouble.

He felt rough, his head swam and a feeling of nausea swept over him. He pulled in to rest for a while. 'Where the hell could he go?' His ribs hurt like mad and all his instincts told him that he should go to hospital, but that was too dangerous. The brothers would soon put the word out and find him. Also, his old colleagues were probably looking for him by now over the petrol bomb attack. 'But where could he go?' He couldn't go to any of his old police friends because that would put them in an impossible position. But he had to disappear until he recovered his health - he wasn't fit for anything in his present state.

It must have been the combination of Wimbledon, where he had stopped, and the urgent need for nursing that gave him the answer in a flash. 'Tracey! Yes, Tracey.' His ex-wife had bought a flat in Wimbledon and he had driven past it once, after their divorce, out of idle curiosity. 'It would be ideal. But would she want to see him again, especially looking the way he did, and would she help?' He argued the pros and cons with himself. They had parted amicably enough, without any bad feelings, and she was a nursing sister. 'I've got no choice' he finally decided 'I'll give it a try.'

Feeling slightly better now that he had made the decision, he drove purposefully towards his ex-wife's flat. Finding an inconspicuous place to park, he settled down to wait until dusk when she should return. When they had parted, she was working regular days so, with any luck, she should be at home during the evening. The flats were more correctly termed luxury flats. They stood in their own grounds, a group of four blocks, three storeys high, each consisting of six flats. The outside decor was mock Tudor. All the flats and houses in this particular area were built in the same style and were managed and maintained by a large property company.

It was approaching dusk when Johnny left the car and made his way stealthily up the staircase at the rear of the flats to the top. The effort required was considerable, he had stiffened up during the long wait in the car, and he leaned against the wall at the top to recover with perspiration running down his smoke-blackened face. As far as he could tell, no-one had seen him enter or climb the stairs.

He drew a deep breath and pressed the bell. After several anxious seconds, he heard footsteps and then a figure appeared behind the door, clearly visible through the small glass panel. 'Who is it?' queried a tentative female voice, curious as to who could be calling at this time - and at the back door.

Johnny heaved a sigh of relief, the figure had looked like Tracey and the voice confirmed it.

'It's OK, love' he replied as calmly as possible 'It's Johnny.'

A bolt was drawn and then slowly the door opened slightly, still on the chain.

The light from the inside fell on Johnny's face. Tracey gave out a cry, half-frightened at the sight, and worried at the state of Johnny, who was barely recognisable.

Quickly she slipped the chain and opened the door wide.

'Hello Tracey' said Johnny, managing a half smile. 'Sorry to disturb you like this ...' His knees buckled, he twisted sideways and fell through the doorway into the kitchen. Only a quick move by Tracey prevented his face from crashing on to the floor. Used to dealing with emergencies, she quickly pulled him into the room and closed the door. 'God, what a mess he looks' she thought as she felt his heartbeat and tested his pulse. He wasn't drunk - clearly whatever he had been up to had stretched him to the limit, until finally his system had rebelled.

She dragged him expertly along the floor and into her bedroom. In no time he was stripped of his clothes and washed, the hardened blood on his swollen face proving particularly stubborn. Then she patched up his visible wounds, applying a wide strapping to the area around his ribs and kidneys which was bruised and inflamed.

She found herself worrying about him and at the same time was angry that she felt this way. After all, she hadn't laid eyes on him since they had split up, and now he had turned up like this - all smashed up. It was just the same as it always was when they were married. He would go out on special jobs, in the middle of the night, usually with the Squad, and return home injured, sometimes via the hospital. In the end it had proved too much for her and the marriage.

But it hadn't been all bad - they had had some terrific times together, especially in the early days. She softened, deciding to wait and hear him out.

Almost as if he could read her thoughts, Johnny stirred, opened his eyes and focussed on his ex-wife standing over him. He managed another half smile and mumbled 'Sorry to be such a bloody nuisance, Tracey. Can you get rid of the old Rover - dump it at a tube station - I don't want anyone to know I'm here.'

'Oh Johnny, what have you been up to this time?' she asked anxiously, but the request fell on deaf ears - he had passed out again.

'Don't want anyone to know I'm here' she repeated out loud "get rid of the old Rover - dump it at a tube station." Damn you Johnny Spencer, who the hell do you think you are?' she said angrily, then when she had calmed down she realised that whatever he wanted she would comply, especially as he was so badly beaten. 'Well, there's nothing for it, I suppose I had better do as he asked. Get rid of the old Rover - but where is it?'

Presuming he had driven there in it, she quickly searched his pockets and found the keys. Pulling on a coat and slipping into a pair of outdoor shoes, she took one last look at Johnny, who was now sleeping peacefully.

'He'll be alright' she said to herself 'He should be out cold for quite a few hours.' Locking the door carefully, she nipped down the back staircase the way he had arrived.

She found the car without difficulty and sitting once more in the comfortable upholstered driver's seat brought memories flooding back. 'Damn you, Johnny Spencer' she repeated out loud, started the engine and pulled away, her eyes full of tears. She blinked back the tears and brought herself back under control 'Dump it at a tube station' he had said. But where? She forced herself to think. He doesn't want anyone to know where he is - therefore he doesn't want to be traced through the car - so any tube station north of the river would be best. She nodded to herself, pleased that at last she had a plan.

She drove over Albert Bridge, all lit up like a fairy-tale bridge, then along the Embankment and left towards Victoria. Then around Hyde Park Corner and northwards in the broad one-way system towards Marble Arch. The traffic was fairly heavy, but moving. No matter what time of the day or night, there was always traffic in this part of London. The Hilton Hotel stood out on her right; followed by the Dorchester, where the uniformed top-hatted doorkeepers could be seen attending to the occupants of Rolls Royces and similar large cars as they queued up outside - there must be a banquet on tonight.

All of a sudden, a startling thought occurred to Tracey 'What if they, whoever they were, whoever Johnny was hiding from, were actually looking for this car - now!' She gripped the wheel tightly - fear registering within her for the first time. She was normally a very cool customer and it took a lot to shake her. In her profession as a nursing sister in charge of a busy casualty department, she was used to seeing every day the results of what one human being was capable of doing to another. Whether by accidents at work, in motor vehicles, intentionally in the furtherance of crime or as a result of one human being reaching breaking point, unable to cope with everyday living in the great Metropolis.

No sooner did this fear possess her, than the solution presented itself. On the left, nearing the Marble Arch area, a sign loomed up 'Parking below. Room for 1,000 cars.'

'That's it, she thought - I can leave the car down there, it could be days before anyone discovers it.' She quickly changed gear, turned the wheel hard left and drove down the ramp. Accepting a ticket from the machine, she drove once round the inside, selected a spot in the darkest corner, and parked. Locking the car, she made her way briskly out of the car park and into the long, tiled tunnel which led to the Marble Arch tube station.

After buying a ticket, she took the Central Line to Notting Hill Gate and changed to the District Line bound for Wimbledon. Only when she was on this train did she allow herself to relax, knowing that Wimbledon was at the end of the line. She felt quite pleased with herself - Johnny had wanted the car dumped at a tube station and she felt that she had gone one better, not only near a tube station, but well hidden from view.

## CHAPTER ELEVEN

The police interview at the hospital with the Steadman brothers finally came to an end. It had been acutely embarrassing for the brothers. Through no fault of their own, they had found themselves, within hours of release from prison, being interviewed by police and, truthfully for a change, they were unable to throw any light on their father's accident. They had, however, promised themselves that before long they would find out just what the hell was going on. They had accompanied the police officers to the mortuary and formally identified the body. The sight of his old battered face, stitched and cleaned up as neatly as possible in the short time available, did nothing to the emotions of his two sons. They had long ceased to worry about what their father did or thought. They did, however, take the fact that his death had been caused deliberately as a direct slight against them. That was something entirely different and some bastard was going to pay for that, make no mistake about it.

Back in the Ward Sister's office once more, the doctor completed various formalities with the brothers and they asked if they could see Claire.

'Certainly' he replied 'but she has been given a sedative, so I don't know if she will be awake or not.' He led the way down the corridor to the room where she had been treated. They entered quietly, followed by the young nurse who had joined them. Claire really was asleep although, unknown to those present, it had only been for a matter of minutes. She had made it back to the hospital in the waiting cab in record time, urging the driver all the time to go faster, until he remarked jokingly 'Blimey lady, what's the panic, you don't look as if you are about to give birth.'

On arrival at the hospital, she had thrust several notes into his hand and dashed up the steps. Composing herself as she passed the receptionist, she flew along the corridor, praying all the time that her absence had not been noticed. Pausing at the end, she glanced carefully round the corridor which led to her room. Good! There was no sign of the doctor or the young nurse who had attended to her. Out of breath and almost fainting with exhaustion and fear, she slipped into the room, closing the door behind her with a sigh of relief. With trembling hands she stripped off her outdoor clothes, terrified that any moment the door would open to admit her brothers. Thankfully she collapsed into bed. Against all the odds, she had tricked them. Within seconds she was asleep, a faint smile of satisfaction still lingering on her pale, worried face.

She didn't hear the doctor say to her brothers 'I think it would be advisable for her to stay for a couple of hours - she seemed pretty exhausted to me.'

'Yes, alright Doc. We'll telephone later' replied Vic adding 'Thanks for your help.'

As they walked away down the corridor, Vic said 'We're going to finish the job we started with that bastard Spencer.'

Then, indicating with his fingers, he counted 'First, there's the petrol bomb - then the brakes on the old man's bleedin' van and third, there's Spencer shacked up with our bloody sister.' He paused 'He's got to know something about it - and we're going to make him talk this time, Billy Boy.' His eyes half closed and the corners of his mouth turned down as he visualised the pleasure it would give him.

'Yes, but I want a chance too, Vic – it's usually my side of the business, you know that' the younger brother complained bitterly.

'Don't worry, Billy, you'll get your chance – don't worry.'

They picked up a cab which had brought someone to the hospital. Driving out of the grounds they both noticed Claire's car parked exactly where they had left it.

Within minutes, they were back at the florist shop. Vic paid off the cabby and they made their way quickly round to the back of the mews.

'Did you get Claire's key, Vic?' asked Billy.

'No, I didn't, but the door shouldn't be too difficult' he grinned. To Vic, doors could be opened in many subtle ways and he had made a speciality of it. The challenge of opening a lock without a key had always given him a chance to show off. He maintained that it required nerve and skill to pick a lock - both things he had always tried to cultivate and, only when all civilised efforts had been attempted, did he call on Billy to use his brute strength.

Vic tried the handle - the door opened.

'That's funny' said Billy 'I thought I saw Claire lock that door.'

''You did, stupid – someone's been in here.' Vic's cutting voice had a mixture of annoyance and disbelief, coupled with a gut feeling that all was not well.

They entered silently and slowly opened the cellar door - the room was empty.

Pieces of cord, deep red where they had been saturated in blood – Spencer's blood - lay on the floor beside the pole.

'Shit - shit – shit' exploded Vic, lashing out with his foot, sending one of the crates flying across the room. 'One of us should have stayed with him' he smashed his fist into his other hand.

Billy picked up the pieces of cord and examined them closely.

'They've been cut clean, Vic - someone must have set him free' his face showing childlike astonishment.

'It's my bleedin' fault, Billy. I should have known that he was bound to have had some kind of back-up. Seeing him with Claire, I just naturally thought he was alone. I should have known' he repeated, his eyes narrowing again 'But I doubt if he's gone far, we can soon put the word about to find him. It shouldn't be too difficult - should it?'

\*\*\*\*\*\*

Tracey entered her flat the way she had left, quietly and unobserved via the back entrance, locking and bolting the door behind her. She hurried to her room and heaved a sigh of relief on finding Johnny sleeping peacefully. Closing the door quietly, she re-entered the neat well-appointed kitchen and made herself a cup of coffee. Taking it through to the lounge, she sat down in a large armchair to wait for Johnny to come out of his sleep.

After a couple of hours, her patience was exhausted and she opened the bedroom door and looked in. This time the little noise she had made was enough to wake him. He opened his eyes and stared at her, unable to figure out for the moment where he was and why he was in his ex-wife's bedroom. He tried to sit up but with a cry of pain fell back again cursing. The excruciating pain in his ribs and his swollen face and lips quickly sent the events of the last twenty-four hours flooding back to him.

Tracey moved briskly towards him, crying out 'Keep still, Johnny - keep still' her eyes full of tenderness and concern. She adjusted his pillow to make him more comfortable.

'Hello, love' said Johnny huskily, managing a half smile 'Sorry to turn up like the proverbial bad penny.'

'Oh Johnny' she whispered 'what is going on, how did you get those injuries?'

'I'll survive' he replied 'I've had worse than this - I think it's only a cracked rib. Thanks for the strapping - a most professional job, if I may say so.'

Tracey replied angrily 'Think yourself lucky, Johnny Spencer, you could easily have punctured a lung. You should still have that lot x-rayed.'

'Yes, yes, I know' he replied seriously 'but it's out of the question at the moment. The main thing is, love, can I hide here for a few days till I can move more easily? And I really mean hide from everyone?'

She thought for several moments and then answered seriously 'Johnny, I'll hide you on one condition.'

'Yes, what's that?'

'That you tell me everything - everything that you've been up to - starting with how you came to get your wrists in that terrible condition. You've obviously been tied up – why, Johnny, why?'

He looked at his wrists, which ached under the clean white bandaging, his lacerated skin and flesh still burning from the antiseptic lotion which she had skilfully applied. His first reaction was to try and bluff it out, but the sight of Tracey standing over him, her eyes showing a mixture of anxiety and stubbornness, made him change his mind. He recognised only too well from their married days the mood she was in and he realised that he was beaten - he had no alternative. With a shrug, he gave in as gracefully as possible, saying with a smile 'OK love, you win, I'll tell you everything, but could I have a cup of something first? My throat and mouth feel foul.'

'Alright, I'll fix you some soup' she said and left the room quickly. Johnny heaved a sigh of relief. So far so good, but how much could he tell her. From past experience he knew that bullshit wouldn't work on Tracey - she was far too clever. 'I can tell her about Smithy and the way I started it all. But can I tell her about Claire?'

Tracey appeared with a tray containing a bowl of soup, some bread and a cup of coffee. She placed the tray down on the bedside table and helped Johnny to sit up. Then picking up the tray again, she placed it in front of him and sat down on the end of the bed. She hadn't spoken since entering the room. Now she looked fully at him and, as if she had read his thoughts said, in a firm 'Sister-on-the-ward' voice, 'Don't give me any of your bullshit, Johnny Spencer, I want the truth or nothing at all.'

Johnny nodded in agreement. Between mouthfuls of soup and questions from Tracey, when he hadn't been specific enough, he related the full story.

She was horrified. 'Surely you should contact your old colleagues in the CID? It's their job, not yours.' Flushed and angry, she continued 'You came out of the Force disgusted with all this sort of thing - remember!'

'I know that, but you forget I started it all. I've got to finish it for Albert's sake.'

She wasn't convinced 'And you think it's worth getting yourself killed for, do you?'

There was no reply. Johnny could not resist the logic of her argument any longer. He closed his eyes and collapsed back onto the pillow, genuinely exhausted.

# CHAPTER TWELVE

The post-mortem on old Bobby Steadman revealed that he had died before going head first through the windscreen and crashing into the base of the tree. A massive heart attack in the last few seconds, as he had summoned up all his reserves to control the brakeless runaway van, had finally overloaded his ageing system.

To the brothers, this fact did nothing to soften the blow - as far as they were concerned, the person or persons who had cut the brake cable were responsible for his death - and they would be dealt with accordingly. The police could make whatever enquiries they liked - the brothers would carry out their own investigations.

A week later, only a few people attended the funeral, mainly relatives and a few of the old gang; the presence of the brothers had certainly deterred some. But if the numbers were few, the floral tributes were many and certainly in keeping with a typical cockney stallholder's funeral. And, as always, in order that the marvellous flowers would not be wasted, arrangements had been made for them to be taken afterwards to the local old folks' home - old Bob would have liked that.

The crematorium service was brief, the coffin looked tiny, hardly large enough to contain the battered body of the old man.

Claire was dressed completely in black, a heavy net veil hiding her eyes and face and hiding the ravages of the past few days. She was supported by a favourite aunt and sobbed afresh as the coffin slid silently backwards on shiny metal rollers.

The plaintive organ music reached a crescendo as the blue silk curtains, adorned with gold braid, swished together and completely hid the coffin from view. The solemn lilting tones of the minister brought the service to an end.

The brothers Vic and Billy, soberly and smartly dressed - after all they had their own reputations to think of - remained stony-faced and unmoved. They were anxious, for reasons of their own, to get the ceremony over and to return to the house.

Filing out, they shook hands, curtly thanked the minister, made a brief tour of the magnificent wreaths, quickly entered the first funeral car and were gone.

It fell to Claire, still supported by her aunt, to thank those who had attended and were not returning to the house. Her duty completed, she sank gratefully into the luxurious seating of the second limousine and relaxed for the first time that day.

Ten minutes later, much more composed, she walked up the neat pathway and entered the house, in which she had spent the greater part of her life. If one discounted the brothers, the house held many happy memories for her. Now, it held nothing for her - first her mother and now her father were gone. She had no ties and could proceed with her own plans to emigrate.

In the living-room, Vic and Billy, with their jackets off, top shirt buttons open and ties pulled aside, had already started drinking - each clutched a large whisky.

'God, how I hate those two' she thought and, avoiding their eyes as much as possible, she made her way quickly up to her bedroom to freshen up. She could hear the sounds outside the house of cars arriving, doors slamming and people entering the house. Good people most of them, old friends of her father.

Anxious not to let old Bob down, she patched up her ravaged face, tidied her hair and after breathing deeply several times to calm her nerves, rejoined the others downstairs. Relatives had rallied round and prepared enough sandwiches for an army, her aunt had boiled the kettle and was busy dispensing tea to those who wanted it, although others made the most of it and got stuck into the beers and shorts.

Vic watched his guests closely and, when those whom he was particularly interested in had settled themselves and consumed a plate of food and drink, he stood up. Billy, as usual, immediately followed suit. Vic passed amongst them saying a few words and indicating, with a movement of his head, the room in which he wished them to congregate. Wives watched anxiously as their husbands followed Vic's instructions, worried at what the outcome might be, yet not daring to interfere. All except one, a brash confident blond called Dolly Wilson, who pleaded loudly for her husband Dave not to go; she knew how lucky they were that he hadn't joined the brothers on their last spell in prison, as he had managed to get away with it through lack of evidence.

Dave, embarrassed by his wife's outburst, followed the others, pausing only to throw gruffly over his shoulder 'Leave it out, Dolly, will-yer.'

The door closed behind them. Vic, with Billy beside him, stood with his back to the old-fashioned marble fireplace. The grate, surrounded by polished brass fender and fire-set, stood empty. The room was the original front parlour. Old Bobby had kept it that way since his wife's death. When everyone had settled, Vic spoke. He related, in a quiet determined fashion, the situation he had found at Claire's flat on their release from prison, giving details of the fire and how Johnny Spencer had been discovered on the premises. Only when he mentioned Spencer did his expression and tone change to one of hatred and bitterness. One or two of those present felt a wave of fear pass up their backs and necks. It was quite obvious, even at this stage, that there was so much hatred consuming Vic after his years inside that, whatever the outcome of this meeting, violence would be called for.

Vic ended by telling them about the tampering of the brakes on his father's van and left those present in no doubt that he intended hunting down those responsible and dealing with them. He called for their assistance to track down Johnny Spencer and to use every means at their disposal to discover who was behind the petrol bomb and the death of his 'old man'. Vic answered various questions, one of which was 'Who do you reckon yourself, Vic?' Various names were suggested, Dace the bookmaker being one of them. Billy confined himself to nodding in agreement.

'Being family and friends, I expect you all to help with information' continued Vic 'It's your contacts and your experience I want you to use at this stage. Muscle I can get anytime.'

Dave Wilson, who had been quiet until then, spoke up 'Vic, I been thinking.'

'I should bloody well hope so' retorted Vic icily 'You didn't have to spend your time locked up with us, did you?'

Dave agreed, continuing 'Alright Vic, look it may be something, it may be nothing, but you mentioned Johnny Spencer and amongst those other names, one was bookie Dace wasn't it?'

'Yes, yes' interrupted Vic impatiently 'get to it - what are you saying?'

Dave swallowed hard and, in a shaking voice, said 'Well, I 'eard a buzz that old Smithy, the tic-tac man who works for Dace, used to be a snout for Spencer when he was in the 'old bill'. I dunno if it's true, but that's what I 'eard.'

'Good – good' replied Vic, a smile appearing on his cruel face for the first time 'That's the kind of thing I want - anybody else heard that?'

There was no confirmation, most of them justified their fears by thinking 'Well, if he was a snout, he deserves all he's going to get.' They shook their heads and began to imagine what would happen to poor old Smithy when the brothers checked the accuracy of this information.

Vic, satisfied for the moment, followed by Billy, led the way back into the main room, some of the wives looking anxiously at their husbands.

******

On the day after Bobby Steadman's funeral there was a meeting between Claire and her brothers at the family house, which she had kept away from as much as possible since they had come out of prison. She had her father's will, which she started to read out. Apart from some pieces of his late wife's jewellery which was left to Claire, the rest of the estate was to be divided equally between the three of them.

Vic and Billy nodded - it was what they had expected. 'Does that include the garages and the land?' queried Vic.

'I was coming to that' replied Claire 'When you two went to prison, someone had to look after your father, pay all the bills and look after this house. He wanted to stay here and said how much he missed not going up to Covent Garden every day.'

'Get to it' interrupted Vic impatiently.

'Well, he suggested that it would be a good idea to start a florist shop together, so that he could continue to go up to the market every morning and, instead of buying fruit and veg, he would buy flowers and I would run the shop.'

'And?' said Vic loudly.

'So he sold the garages and land to finance the shop and flat and, when it took off, he agreed to let me have the shop instead of my third share in the whole of his estate. But he didn't get round to including this in the will before he died.'

'But you just said that everything was to be split three ways' said Vic angrily.

'Yes I know - but I feel that with the shop and flat I've got my share and I have no intention of claiming anything more.'

'What does all this mean, Vic?' queried Billy.

'It means that our crafty sister has fixed herself up nicely with a flat and a business while we've been away and according to the will she is still entitled to a third of the house – that's what it means Billy. She says she's had her third but I'm not happy.'

Claire fought back 'I can't help it if you two weren't here when the sale went through - anyway Dad was the one who took the opportunity to buy the garages and land in the first place when they were going cheap - you didn't contribute anything towards it.'

'Well I'm still not happy about it - you could easily change your mind. I'm going to call the solicitor and get him to contest the will. He's the one to sort this lot out. And then what about the arches?'

'Well you know he didn't own them and only rented them and the lease runs out soon, so if you want to keep them going you'll have to renegotiate a new one yourselves.'

'Despite all your education you haven't made much of a success of it' sneered Vic. Inwardly, Claire praised herself for having kept the two sets of accounts going and she fought back, saying 'And look what's happened to my business since you two came out of prison. I haven't got any enemies, so everything that's happened has got to be down to you. It also means that from now on you'll have to pay your own way, all my money has gone on the funeral and the reception.'

'You seem to forget that we caught you with that bastard Spencer. Things also started to go wrong when he appeared on the scene, didn't they? Somebody could have been after him, he's made enough enemies in his time and now he's disappeared - even his mates can't find him, so I've heard.'

Vic wasn't finished yet, adding 'But you won't have to worry will you?' he sneered 'The insurance money will cover the damage and the place could do with a face lift anyway - you might even get a few more customers.'

Claire played them along, saying 'That may be so, but it'll be some time before that can happen and I'll have to borrow some money to keep things ticking over. It won't be easy - just be thankful, at least you've got a roof over your heads.'

Claire had had enough, she was anxious to be as far away from her brothers as possible. Leaving them, she replied hotly 'Talk to your solicitor by all means, but don't come to me for any more money because I'm broke.' This wasn't strictly true as she had made ample provision for this day and there was no way that her brothers were getting their hands on it.

****** 

'Billy! Claire, the crafty bitch, has put us in the picture regarding the house and I've made an appointment to see the solicitor. But we are really short of the readies. We're going to have to put the pressure on somewhere.'

'What about that Chinese bloke, Chin, he was always good for a few notes wasn't he?'

'Yes, that's right, till that bastard Spencer stepped in and protected him.' Vic paused for thought and said slowly 'But he's not around anymore is he? It's certainly worth a try. Well done, Billy.'

Billy's chest stuck out and he smiled stupidly at the praise from his brother. The thought that he might be called upon to use his strength on someone or something appealed to him greatly.

'Get in touch with Dave, he can drive us. They always do well at the Chinese on a Saturday night so there should be plenty to tide us over till we can make arrangements for the future.'

That evening saw the brothers and Dave Wilson in his car, watching the restaurant from a darkened alley close by. It was late and only a few customers remained. Eventually they left and they could see Chin saying goodnight to them on the doorstep. He was about to lock up when Billy's large boot prevented him, as he pushed himself through the doorway followed by Vic and Dave.

'Sorry, we're closed' cried Chin anxiously, immediately expecting trouble.

'Hello Chin' said Vic brightly 'Long time no see.'

'Meester Steadman' said Chin, his voice wavering 'What you wan?'

'Just thought we would pay you a little visit for old time's sake. You can tell your wife and son to come out from the kitchen now.'

Chin did as he was told and, as they appeared, Vic signalled for them to sit at one of the tables.

Vic smiled and looking round the restaurant said 'You seem to be doing very well Chin, everywhere looks great. I like all those mirrors and that well-stocked fish tank, it would be a pity if one of those Chinese Dogs happened to smash into them.' He smiled again, leaving Chin in no doubt that Billy would be only too pleased to make it happen.

'No need for that, Meester Steadman' pleaded Chin, repeating his original question 'What you wan?'

'We'll start with what's in the till' replied Vic, nodding to Billy who moved quickly across the room and with one large finger made the till spring open to display the night's considerable takings.

At this Chin's son leapt to his feet, his mother grabbed his arm to pull him down saying 'Don't interfere son, keep out of it.'

'That's very good advice, sonny boy. I should take it if you know what's good for you.'

Chin's son Lee was tall and well built and was also a black belt Judo player and quite able to look after himself, but reluctantly he sat down again saying 'Get the police, Dad, they sorted this lot out the last time they were after money.'

'Your boy's got a lot to say for himself, Chin, and that kind of talk could get him in a lot of trouble, but I'm glad to see that you've got him under control' said Vic, warming to the task.

Billy had started to make a move towards the son, when Vic said 'No, no, Billy, your job is to empty that till. This cocky boy can wait,' thus preventing what could have been a most interesting confrontation. Billy's streetwise bulk against a skilful Judo player.

So Billy did as he was told and started stuffing the notes into his pockets as fast as he could.

Vic grabbed Chin by the front of his coat which he twisted viciously, saying 'And this is just on account. When we call next Saturday I expect you to have at least a grand for us. That'll give you plenty of time to get it together - you understand?'

Chin, who was sweating profusely, pleaded 'Meester Steadman, we don't make that kind of money - please. I have staff to pay.'

'Don't give me that crap, Chin. I've seen how well you do - just have the money and ignore your son's advice. Remember - Spencer is no longer in the police to help you out this time.'

Grasping at straws, Chin said 'But that Meester Buller, he come in here quite often and he may come in again.'

'Yes, if he does and you tell him of our visit, you and your family will be in big trouble' snarled Vic, twisting the coat tighter and causing Chin to gasp for air, saying 'Alright, alright – I understand.'

'You'd better, if you know what's good for you' uttered Vic, releasing the coat and pushing Chin away from him roughly.

'Right boys, we'll leave our friends to consider the proposition.' Vic turned and headed for the door followed by his two henchmen.

In the car heading for home, Billy handed over the notes which Vic quickly counted. 'They did have a good night, there's nearly four hundred quid here. And not a bad night for us either, considering there was no aggravation.'

Billy, who was disappointed about that, said 'Yes, but that son of Chin's is a bit cocky. I think we need to keep an eye on him.'

'Just you leave the thinking to me, Billy boy. You'll get a chance of some action before long, don't worry.'

\*\*\*\*\*\*

The following Saturday night saw Vic and Billy in Dave Wilson's car again in the alleyway outside Chin's restaurant.

'Do you think Chin will call the law after our visit last week?' queried Billy.

'No chance. I think I put the shits up Chin enough to prevent him from doing that' Vic replied confidently 'As you can see, everything looks normal.'

Soon Chin was seeing his last customer off the premises and almost immediately Billy pushed his way in, followed closely by Vic and Dave.

Chin stood some way away from Vic this time, looking worried, his eyes moving from side to side, sweat already breaking out on his brow. All seemed quiet in the room. 'Well, Chin' demanded Vic 'You got the money?'

'Yes, Meester Steadman, I got the money – and I'm keeping it' he said, moving quickly away from Vic.

Before Vic could respond, six Judo players, all Chinese, appeared from behind various screens at different parts of the room. They were wearing Judo suits complete with their belts, several of which were black. They all adopted a defensive pose with their hands up. One of them was the son, Lee, who had a confident, defiant look on his face.

An elderly man who appeared to be their leader spoke in a firm voice 'Meester Steadman, we are sportsmen and we come in peace to protect our friend Mr. Chin and to give you a friendly warning.'

Vic already had his knife out and was switching it from hand to hand in a threatening manner and Billy looked stupidly at his brother for help. This was a situation neither of them had come across before. They didn't know what to make of it.

The leader spoke again 'As I said before, we come in peace but we could easily come armed with meat cleavers, if you would rather have it that way' he bowed and smiled as he said this.

Vic looked menacingly at Chin, saying 'You don't know what a fuckin' chance you and your friends are taking here – I can easily wait.'

'You tell me not to tell the police – I obey you – these men are my friends.'

The leader spoke up again 'Steadman, the whole of the Chinese community in the area have been told to watch you. Come anywhere near Chin and his family and you have all of us to deal with. Understand? Now I think you had better leave.'

Vic realised that the situation was not in his favour. Usually the odds were very much the other way and he had no idea how well Billy could handle himself against these Judo experts, so he decided that retreat was the best option under the circumstances.

'Come on Billy, we're leaving. You haven't heard the last of this, Chin. Just watch your back.'

They turned to leave with the words, this time loudly and in unison from the Judo group 'And you watch yours, Steadman' ringing in their ears.

Before they had reached the door, it suddenly burst open and in came the formidable figure of Detective Inspector Buller followed closely by Detective Sergeant Read and another CID sergeant.

Vic swung round to Chin, saying 'I warned you not to get the law involved.'

'He didn't have to, Steadman' boomed Buller 'I've heard it said that you boast that you know everything that goes on in this manor, even when you're in prison. Well, believe it or not, I get to know about everything that goes on my manor too and I heard that something was going off tonight. Although I didn't think it was going to be in fancy dress – you should have warned me' he grinned 'Anyone care to enlighten me as to what's going on?'

The Judo leader was the first to reply, 'Nothing to worry about, Mr. Buller. We're just having a little get-together. The food is very good here.'

'And you have to dress up in your Judo outfits to do this? Pull the other leg, it plays Annie Laurie. So what's really going on, Chin?'

'These men are members of my son's Judo club and he invited them for a meal.'

'And I suppose he invited the Steadman gang as well, did he?' said Buller, who, looking at Vic, said 'I can guess what's going on here, you two have been out of prison for some weeks now and I haven't heard of any robberies or heists taking place in this neck of the woods, so you must be getting short of cash and you're up to your old tricks again.'

'You've got it all wrong, Buller' spat Vic. 'I imagine that bastard Spencer, who put us away, has got something to do with this.'

'He's no longer in the Force, thanks to you, and he's got nothing to do with this.'

'Maybe – but he's still got a big mouth. He stitched us up and got away with it which wasn't surprising, you lot always protect your own.'

Vic, conscious of the fact that he still had his knife on him, tried to keep Buller talking. 'Why do you think Spencer has disappeared then? Nobody seems to know where to find him, so he must be well hidden.'

'Alright Steadman, it looks as if we got here just in time and there doesn't appear to have been any damage done, so I suggest that the three of you get on your way. But remember, we will be watching you.'

Vic, realising that he had pushed Buller as far as he dared, took the opportunity to leave and, followed by Billy and Dave, headed quickly for the car.

Buller turned to the Judo leader and said 'Which leaves me with you lot. I can well imagine why you're here and it seems to have worked out for you, but be very careful in the future. I will not stand for any vigilante groups operating on my manor. So just take this as a friendly warning. But well done – it's a change for someone to put one over the Steadman brothers.' He smiled and showed his bad teeth, visible even in the subdued light of the restaurant. 'So, Chin. Have you any complaint you wish me to look into?'

'No, no, Meester Buller. All settled now.'

'Alright, but if you do see Spencer, tell him I'd like a word with him. I know that he used to come in here and his name has come up recently in connection with a fire.'

'Yes, yes, I will,' agreed Chin, anxious to get Buller off the premises.

Buller and his colleagues left and Chin locked the door securely behind them. Turning to those left behind, he clapped his hands, saying 'Thank you, thank you, everybody. Now let's all have a drink to celebrate a good night's work.'

# CHAPTER THIRTEEN

'So the poor bugger snuffed it then' mumbled the deep throaty voice, puffing out a long stream of cigar smoke, which was soon lost amid the stale pall already clinging to the darkened ceiling. The hand which held the large cigar had fingers which were almost as fat; one of them sported a huge sovereign ring with a ruby set in the middle. It was flash, just like the rest of the person, who was overweight and over-dressed, with a dark-red carnation in his button hole and a matching silk handkerchief in his top pocket. Across the wide expanse of his stomach stretched an old-fashioned gold watch chain on the end of which was a real gold Hunter - possible the only item of taste on the whole body. The watch had been accepted by Terrance 'Lucky'

Dace, the bookmaker, in settlement of a gambling debt, which some unfortunate punter had been unable to honour.

He was seated, whisky glass in hand, in the corner of the lounge bar of 'The Sportsman', his favourite pub, with two of his henchmen. Dace felt that the name of the pub suited his image. The irony of the situation was that the atmosphere in the place would have had any real sportsman clamouring for the exit.

The person who had just delivered the news of Bobby Steadman's death couldn't have contrasted more with Dace. His name was Tommy Stock and he was in his forties, dark-skinned and with a thick crop of prematurely grey hair. In a way it made him look distinguished but such an idea was dashed, however, as soon as he opened his mouth. He was the hard man of the outfit, lean, quick and vicious. Even his friends avoided having to look into his cold grey eyes. He was always introduced as one of Lucky Dace's business associates which, amongst other things, is what he was. In practice, he was Dace's minder. He helped Dace run his three betting shops, assisted him at the race tracks whenever he set up his board, and had the reputation of being a very reliable hitman - if the price was right.

Completing the trio was Dace's brother-in-law Poxy Huston, who was shorter than the other two, stocky and muscular but not too bright. The term 'built like a brick shithouse' could have been coined especially for Poxy. His face was deeply pitted and marked, particularly around one eye. He had acquired his nickname, not through ''avin 'ad the pox', as he was always quick to point out, but through a number of pellets from a 10-bore shotgun hitting the side of his face. 'Nearly lost the bleedin' eye' he would say, but what was not readily apparent was that his backside was similarly marked.

Poxy had, in his time, been very agile and athletic. In his youth he had fancied himself as a cat man - he certainly had no fear of heights - or anything else for that matter, but he had been surprised whilst on a country-house job with two others. The owner had returned from a shoot unexpectedly and caught them inside the house. While they were trying to escape, the contents of one barrel had caught the side of his face.

'Thought it had blown me bleedin' 'ead orf' he often said, but then added that the contents of the second barrel had hit him in the backside. Only his superb physical condition and the assistance of his mates, who came back for him, had saved the day. A local doctor had removed the pellets, for a price and with no questions asked but with considerable embarrassment to Poxy. It had been quite some time before he had been able to sit down with comfort.

So the marks around his eye and the side of his face were the penalty he had had to pay for his trip to the gentleman farmer's house. 'Never did like the bleedin' country, anyway' he would add 'dirty, smelly places - give me the Smoke everytime.'

Over the years he had managed to turn his hidden disfiguration to advantage, since his party piece, when he had had a few, and there was enough encouragement, was to remove his shoes, trousers, socks and underpants, usually to the accompaniment of the music of 'The Stripper' shouted out by those buying the drinks and encouraging him. Then he would lift his shirt tail to expose two white cheeks pitted with blue marks. This always went down well with the crowd, who whistled and cheered with enjoyment. In some ways it compensated for the pain and suffering that Poxy had had to contend with and the act certainly took a lot of beating for its entertainment value.

On this night, however, he was sober and his comment on the news of the death of old Bob Steadman was confined to 'Well, he was gettin' on a bit anyway - he probably died of an 'eart attack.' He lowered his voice, looked around and continued in a confidential manner 'There's no way anyone can tie the petrol bottle or the van to any of us.'

'Just make bloody sure it stays that way' interrupted Dace, seriously. The cold grey eyes of Tommy Stock warmed 'We timed it just right, boss' he chuckled 'just before those two bastards were released from the nick.'

'Yeah' mumbled Dace 'Vic Steadman used to boast that he knew everything that was going on on the outside while he was inside. Well this time we knew what was going on inside - like exactly when he was coming out.'

They all laughed loudly, Dace so much that he was seized by a fit of coughing and his huge frame and stomach shook as he turned red in the face. Dabbing his eyes with another silk handkerchief produced like a magician from a side pocket, he enjoyed the joke. The Steadmans had long been a thorn in their sides and they had all been well pleased to see the brothers put away, even if it was true that they had been set up.

When the laughter subsided, Dace continued quietly 'But just to be on the safe side, better keep an eye on those two buggers. See to it, will you Tommy.'

'Sure, boss' he replied 'leave it to me. It'll be a pleasure.'

They continued to drink and chat, happy that they had managed to put one over their much hated rivals, the Steadmans.

As they were leaving 'The Sportsman', Tommy Stock caught up with Poxy.

'Poxy, I reckon the Guvnor's going soft. We ought to be doing a bit more to those Steadmans.'

'Yeah, I agree, but remember he doesn't want us to be tied in with the brakes on the van which killed their old man, or the fire at the florist shop.'

'Well, I'm not happy. I reckon we should do something to put the frighteners on them.'

'As long as it's only that, I agree, but no more bodies – right' said Poxy, well aware of Tommy's reputation.

'Alright, alright, we don't have to kill anybody. Just let them know we're no pushovers. Leave it to me. I've already got an idea of how we can let them know that they can't do just what they like around here. I can get a couple of my mates to do it for me, that way none of us needs to get involved.'

'That sounds good to me, but be careful.'

'You worry too much, Poxy – just leave it to me.'

\*\*\*\*\*\*

Dave Wilson was driving his wife Dolly to the supermarket one morning and, as usual, she was bending his ear.

'You're going to have to get some kind of regular job, we've got kids to feed and clothe, we just 'aven't got enough money coming in. If it wasn't for my cleaning jobs, we'd really be in the shit.'

'I've given you money when the Steadmans have coughed up, haven't I?'

'Yea, I know, and I wonder how they got 'old of that? Here's you running them around like a bloody taxi business and I'm the one paying the tax and insurance. It doesn't make bloody sense.'

'I know, Dolly, but I owe them, remember. They kept me out of prison, but I've got an idea of how I might be able to get out of their mob. I'm just waiting for the right moment.'

'Well it's going to have to be bloody soon, 'cos I've 'ad enough of it.'

To Dave's relief they had reached the supermarket, he pulled in and parked the car, at least he should get some respite from his wife's tongue whilst pushing the trolley.

After an uneventful shopping session, they were soon on their way home again.

Dave was soon aware that someone was following him. A car had left the car park and was tight on his heels. His interior mirror showed two men wearing dark glasses and caps in a battered old BMW which looked as if it had seen better days. Should he say something to Dolly? 'No' he thought 'it would only start her off again.' The car kept on his tail until he reached a quiet part of the road with hardly any traffic, when without warning, he was struck from behind. Not seriously, more of a nudge. He put his foot down and Dolly said 'What the 'ell's goin' on?'

'It's just a couple of blokes playing silly buggers' replied Dave as they were struck more forcefully from behind, causing both of them to slam hard against their seat belts.

'Well, pull over and I'll have a right go at them' said Dolly, her quick temper rising.

Ignoring his wife's outburst, Dave put his foot down - no way was he going to stop and get out of the car.

The car behind caught them up and again nudged the back of the car, more forcefully this time and then it disappeared down a left-hand turning behind them.

Looking in the mirror, Dave said 'It's alright, they've gone now' and relaxed.

Dolly, however, was not happy 'This 'as got to do with your bloody mates, ain't it?'

'Maybe, no harm done' replied Dave, as he pulled into a garage forecourt.

Dolly continued to rant 'This is someone getting to the Steadmans through you, isn't it?' She paused, her eyes blazing 'Well I've 'ad enough of it, either you leave them or I'll leave you.' Dave sat motionless, he could offer no words of explanation or comfort.

Eventually he drove out of the garage and looked to his right - there was no sign of the car or the two men. On reaching his house he turned and faced Dolly, saying seriously 'I will definitely leave the brothers this time - I'll find a way, I promise.'

## CHAPTER FOURTEEN

'Billy, whichever way you look at it we're still short of the readies. The little we got from the Chinese restaurant helped, but it was never going to be enough. I think it's time to call in a few favours – either that or we're going to have to go back to work again.'

'You talk about calling in a few favours - what about that Brummie lad we helped out in prison. His father sounded as if he would be happy to do us a favour after what we did for his son.'

'Good thinking, you've got your brain in gear at last.'

Billy grinned stupidly at the unaccustomed praise from his brother.

Vic's eyes narrowed as his mind went back to an incident in the shower room in prison when, along with

Billy whose reputation was well known, they had stepped in to prevent a young lad from being shafted by two randy cons. It wasn't because of any noble sentiment on Vic's part – no – it was just that Vic had been grooming the lad himself. It transpired that the lad had a criminal father who lived and worked in Birmingham. He was a successful fence and Vic had thought that he might be a useful contact in the future. The father had phoned Vic and told him how grateful he was for the way that he had looked after his son. The father was a metal dealer whose speciality, Vic had found out, was to make gold and silver change into ingots and then disappear without trace. He had also indicated that perhaps they could do some business together at some time in the future. The son had been released just before Vic and Billy.

Vic's brain was working overtime and after several moments he said 'I've got an idea how we could get our hands on some good silverware and gold coins and maybe settle an old score at the same time.'

'What do you mean?'

'Well I've given a lot of thought as to who could be responsible for cutting the brake wires on the old man's van and causing the fire at our stupid sister's shop and the only outfit capable of pulling a stunt like that has got to be that bookie Dace's lot.'

'Yeah that's right, I never did like them' nodded Billy.

'But at the same time, putting two and two together, there's the answer as to where we could get our hands on some silver and gold.'

'You mean do Dace's house?'

'Yeah, but we'd have to be bloody careful, it would have to be well planned. Also, after that run-in with Buller, he'd be on us like a ton of bricks – and we'd have to have cast iron alibis' he added.

Billy, who was warming to the idea, suggested 'The best time to do the house would be when Dace's lot are all at the dogs in the evening, wouldn't it?'

'Billy, what did you have for breakfast today? That's the second good idea you've had. But we'd have to make sure that there's nobody left in the house at the time. I can handle the alarm but it would save a lot of time if we knew exactly where he keeps his silver and if there are any safes.' Vic thought for moment and then said 'Didn't he have an 'andyman at one time who looked after the garden and did odd jobs - what happened to him?'

'I 'eard that Dace sacked him, said he was an idle bastard and was taking the piss.'

'Find out who that was and arrange for us to meet him, will you, but be very careful. Make sure that nobody else gets to hear.'

'Right, that shouldn't be too difficult. I'll get on to it right away.'

\*\*\*\*\*\*

A few days later, in a pub well away from their usual haunts, Vic and Billy met a man called Jones who Billy had managed to track down. Jones appeared nervous and was sweating profusely.

'I understand that you worked for bookie Dace at one time. Is that right?'

'Yeah, but only as a handyman and I did the lawns and garden.'

'So what happened? I heard that Dace sacked you.'

'As you know, Dace is always putting on a show and boasting about his possessions and his wonderful house and garden. OK, he's a successful bookie and he looks after his money. He doesn't piss it up the wall like some of 'em do.'

'So how do you stand with him at the moment?'

'Well, after I got laid off from the railways a couple of years ago, Dace's job suited me down to the ground. It covered me beer money, although I'd be the first to admit I'm no bloody gardener. I've never managed to get a job since.'

'So he's not your favourite man then?'

'You can say that again, but what's all this about?'

'We wondered if you would like to earn yourself a few bob?'

'I sure would, but I know you by reputation. I've never been in any trouble with the law and I don't see what I could do for you.'

'Don't worry, it's only information that we want.'

Jones heaved a sigh of relief and asked 'What kind of information?'

'I take it you're familiar with the inside of Dace's house as well as the garden?'

'Yeah, he had me doing all sorts of jobs inside, including making tea and coffee.'

'What about the silverware?'

'Oh, yeah. Sometimes I had to help that sister of his to polish his bleedin' candlesticks - and that wasn't my job either' he grumbled.

'OK, cards on the table. Would you be able to give us a detailed plan of where he keeps all his silver and his gold coins?'

'Bloody 'ell, you're going to do the place' he gasped.

'Does that worry you?'

'No - not as long as I'm well out of the frame when it happens.'

'Look, we managed to find out that Dace had sacked you, so there is the possibility that the law will get to know that and come looking for you. How do you feel about that?'

'I'll have to make sure I've got a cast iron alibi for when you're doing it and then I reckon I can hold my own with the plod' he grinned.

'Little does he know what it's like to be interrogated by someone like Buller' thought Vic.

'What are we talking about in notes?' asked Jones, suddenly more confident.

'Don't worry, you'll get your share' said Vic 'depending how well the job goes. The main thing is that you've never had any dealings with us and you stick to that. Right, we've got pen and paper but I think it would be better if we find a quiet spot in the car and you can draw up the plan of the house and garden and where the alarm is.'

All three got up and made their way to where Dave Wilson was waiting in his car. After a short drive they parked in a quiet side road and settled down to draw up the plan and quiz Jones as to every last detail regarding the house which would be useful to them.

\*\*\*\*\*\*

The following Saturday night saw Vic and Billy in a hired van, which had been fitted with false plates, with Dave behind the wheel. They were keeping an eye on

Dace's large detached house, which sat well back from the tree-lined road in one of the suburbs, waiting for Dace and his minder to leave for the dogs. They had sussed out the house as much as they could without drawing attention to themselves and, together with the plan provided by Jones, they felt confident enough to break in.

Eventually, they saw Poxy Huston arrive on foot, collect the keys from the house and drive the Daimler from the garage. He waited on the drive till Dace appeared, locked his front door, and entered the car. They then headed off towards Wimbledon, possibly picking up Tommy Stock on the way.

It was to be a gala night at the dogs and Dace was sure to be there at his favourite spot, calling the odds along with Smithy, his trusty tic-tac man.

Vic and Billy waited for a few minutes, in case Dace had forgotten anything and came back, and then got out of the van and walked to the back of the house where there was a single-lane service road. The van moved off to wait at a place in front of the house where Dave could see and be seen.

Forcing the rear gate lock, they were soon inside the garden and waiting to see if their entry had been noticed. The garden had been tastefully landscaped and Vic could easily imagine why Jones had been sacked, since all this required more than the efforts of a handyman. They made their way towards the house, keeping to a side fence and managed to avoid setting off any alarm or security light. So far, the information provided by Jones was working perfectly. The back door proved easy to deal with and in no time they were both in the house. Vic dealt expertly with the alarm and again they waited to see if their presence had been noticed. Billy's heavy breathing was the only sound to be heard. The light of their torches, taped to allow just a slit of light, showed many silver ornaments, which they collected up and placed in builder-type bags, wrapping them in newspaper to prevent them clinking together. Eventually they found what they were really looking for, a huge leather sofa across one corner of the room. Together they move it forward and raised the carpet to reveal a locked trapdoor in the floor which Vic opened easily. Once opened it revealed a cache of silver – Dace's best silver, which he had collected over the years and only came out when he had his dinner parties to impress the guests. They emptied the contents into the sacks, again quickly wrapping each one.

So far so good, but Jones hadn't been able to tell them where Dace kept his collection of coins and gold – it had to be in a proper safe somewhere. Vic started a concerted search of the room, while Billy began shifting some of the sacks containing the silver to the rear garden door, by the same route by which they had entered. Billy had made several trips successfully but Vic still hadn't found the safe. Time was running out, they wanted to be in the King George pub where their alibis were to be established. Wilson was to shift the loot in the van to the other side of London. In desperation, Vic, trying to put himself in Dace's mind, noticed an elaborate drinks cabinet, which didn't seem to fit flush to the wall. He ran his fingers around the top and sides and found a slight gap. He eased the cabinet round and revealed the safe set into the wall. Pausing only to give a thumbs-up to Billy, who was getting very impatient because he felt that they had been in the house too long and was anxious to get away, Vic set about doing what he was famous for - opening safes. His reputation proved true and, after several attempts, the door swung open. Reaching inside, he pulled out a slim leather case and, after checking its contents, he quickly put it in one of the bags and signalled to Billy that they were ready to leave. Pausing only to signal to Dave with a torch from a front window that he should bring the van around to the back, Vic and Billy left, keeping to the side fence.

The van eased quietly to the back gate. Now was the delicate bit. They had to hope that none of the neighbours had seen or heard them and luck was on their side as they quickly and quietly loaded up the van and jumped inside. Dave slowly eased out to the main road and drove towards the King George.

Stopping only to drop off Vic and Billy at the pub where they were well known, in order to establish their alibis, Dave drove the van carefully northwards and over the river, heading for North West London. He was not a happy man, he could feel himself being gradually sucked into the activities of the brothers more and more, but at the moment he could see no way of extracting himself from the situation. He felt vulnerable, but he could also see the sense in the brothers setting themselves up with decent alibis, as the law would certainly be after them, as it was a job that had their trademark all over it. For the time being he felt fairly confident driving the van as long as he didn't draw attention to himself by speeding or getting involved in an accident.

Finally he arrived at a large, gated scrapyard in an area not too far from Wembley stadium. He could just see the twin towers, although his mind at the moment couldn't have been further from anything to do with football.

Soon he was pulling into a large shed in a retail park, where a refrigerator van was waiting, and two men closed the doors quickly behind him. With the minimum of conversation, the silver and gold was quickly transferred to the other van. In no time, Dave backed his van out and headed back across the Thames, thankful that his part in the operation was over. Shortly the refrigerator van would be heading up the M1 to Birmingham and before the night was out the silver and gold would be melted down, leaving no trace of what it had been or where it had come from.

Vic and Bill seemed happy with their night's work, everything appeared to have gone to plan, no fingerprints left at the house, obviously a lot of planning had gone into the operation. All they had to do was to keep a low profile and wait till the shit hit the fan.

Dave felt a bit happier now, as all he had to do was to change the plates back and deliver the van to one of Vic's associates who would see that it was returned to its rental company. And then he would have to go to the local snooker club to meet several of his mates who would vouch for his having been there all evening. He grinned to himself as he imagined what would happen when bookie Dace returned home to find his precious silver and gold missing.

## CHAPTER FIFTEEN

The last race at Wimbledon Dog Track was over and Dace, in his Daimler with Poxy driving and having dropped Tommy Stock off on the way, was almost home.

It had been a good evening with most of the favourites losing. He had come out on top as usual and, as he relaxed in comfort in the leather upholstery with one of his huge cigars, he felt on top of the world, unaware of what awaited him at home.

The first indication that all was not well was when the alarm didn't go off as he opened his front door. As he had been broken into before, he was immediately suspicious and he waited for Poxy to return from putting the car away before entering. Then he noticed that the security sensor in the hall was not flickering.

'Poxy, it looks as if we've been fuckin' done again.'

He pushed the lounge door open with the knuckle of his index finger, put on the light and saw that the furniture had been moved and in the corner the drinks cabinet stood to one side, showing the safe door wide open. He said angrily 'The bastards have even had my floor safe open as well, which means all my precious silver is gone - some fucker is going to pay for this, believe me.'

'I don't hear any noise from upstairs, let's have a quick look.' When they reached the landing, they looked in the bedrooms, which were tidy and undisturbed.

'At least they haven't trashed the place' said Dace thankfully 'We'd better get the law.' He placed the 999 call and in no time an area car arrived, followed by a CID car driven by Detective Sergeant Read from the local station, who took charge.

'You're not having much luck, Mr Dace' said Read sarcastically 'I hope your business is doing well. It can't be more than a year since I was here the last time.'

'Hello, Sergeant Read, at least you're a friendly face.'

'Detective Inspector Buller is on his way, you'll be glad to hear.'

'Oh no, we didn't exactly hit it off the last time. He likes to throw his weight about too much for me, although I must admit he got a result.'

'Believe me, Mr Dace, you couldn't have anyone better on the case.'

'I know, I know, it's just that he's such an awkward bugger.'

'You know the drill by now. Have you got a copy of all your silver and gold coins which you think have been stolen. I can send it to all police forces straight away and, you never know, we might actually catch someone with it.'

'Yes I have. I keep it for insurance purposes and I admire your optimism.'

Twenty minutes later, Buller appeared, looking even more scruffy than usual – as if he had been having an early night and been dragged out of bed.

'We meet again, Mr. Dace. What's missing this time? Is it valuable silver again? If so, why don't you put it in the bank where it would be safe? If I remember correctly, that's what I advised the last time. I take it that's what's gone again?'

'Yes, you're right, Inspector, although it looks much more serious this time - they've really cleaned me out, all my best silver and the gold.'

'Shall we have a look upstairs?'

'OK, but we've already had a look and it seems OK.'

'Do you mind if we have a look again and then we can see if we only have to seal off this room and maybe the kitchen.'

They went upstairs together and Buller agreed that everything seemed in order.

'That's the first bit of good luck, Mr. Dace, at least you will be able to get a good night's sleep.'

'What, with all this on my mind. You must be joking.'

'Look there's not much more we can do tonight. You've given a complete description of what's missing to Sergeant Read and he has circulated it, so I'll be back with the scene of crimes lot first thing in the morning. I'll see myself out.'

\*\*\*\*\*\*

Buller and Read appeared early the next morning, as promised. They were accompanied by two SOCOs. One, the fingerprint man, was middle-aged, on the portly side, grey-haired and losing it rapidly. The other was younger, slim, much smarter and laden with cameras.

Read, who had already organised house-to-house enquiries before leaving the station, set about taking a statement from Dace about the burglary, while Buller and the photographer concentrated on the lounge. The fingerprint man immediately dealt with the rear kitchen door and frame, in order to get the house back to normal as soon as possible. The dust was soon flying and the rear garden gate would be next on his list.

Buller gave the room a good going-over, hoping to find the slightest clue which might have been left behind by the thieves. All he could find was an area where there was a sandy deposit on the floor and a few scraps of newspaper, which had obviously been used to wrap the silver. Everywhere seemed clean, with no sign of prints anywhere, so obviously they had been wearing gloves.

Buller spoke 'This is no ordinary spur of the moment break-in, it's too well planned, too professional. For somebody to be able to deal with the alarm, plus four locks, as easily as this, it has to be an expert. It's too well planned.'

Dace had joined them by now and Buller continued, 'Have you upset anybody lately? Anybody you've taken a lot of money off lately who might be after squaring the odds.' Dace had already marked down Vic Steadman in his mind as the possible safe man, but was reluctant to accuse him in view of the on-going investigation into the death of old Bobby Steadman and the fire bomb at the sister's shop, which he and his crew had been responsible for.

Getting no response, Buller continued 'These dinner parties that you are famous for, to which it seems you invite half of London. Could there be one or two dodgy characters that might be envious of all your wealth and have sussed out your place while they're here?'

Dace thought for a moment 'I'm pretty sure that it's none of them.'

'So you know all of them personally?'

'Pretty well – yes.'

'Other bookmakers?'

'Yes, that's the game I'm in.'

'In my experience, I'd be surprised if they were all kosher - and it's not the first time you've been done over is it?'

'No, but you dealt with that yourself and none of those who went down for it had anything to do with my parties.'
'That's true' agreed Buller.

Unable to contain himself any longer, Dace blurted out 'Well there's only one name that fits the bill as far as I'm concerned and that's Vic Steadman, he's known to boast that he can open any lock.'

'Yes, but there are plenty of others in London capable of doing this job on your floor safe – you don't have to be a brain surgeon. But don't worry Mr. Dace, I certainly will be having a word with the Steadman brothers along with others.'

\*\*\*\*\*\*

Over the next few days, Buller and his team interviewed all the likely candidates considered for the burglary at Dace's house, without much success. The most interesting interview was the one with the Steadman brothers.

'So, we meet again, Steadman, this is the second time in as many weeks.' These words greeted Vic Steadman as he entered the interview room. Buller and Detective Sergeant Read were seated on one side of a large desk waiting for him. Billy was being held in another room.

'You going soft, Buller?' quipped Vic 'Inviting us to the station – in the old days you would have steamed up to our house at five in the morning, all bells ringing, waking up the neighbourhood to lift us. Probably breaking the door down at the same time.'

'Never mind about that, Steadman, you know why you're here.'

'Course I do, Buller, you've had half the cons in London in here. What I can't understand is why it's taken so long to get round to us?'

'Maybe I've got my own reasons for that, like making a few enquiries beforehand as to what you've been up to lately.'

'And you've come up with nothing' interrupted Vic, fiercely.

'OK, so let's have your version of where you and your brother were last Saturday evening.'

'Not difficult at all, Billy and me had a quiet drink in the George, which you've probably found out already. No?'

'What time did you actually go to the George?'

'It was quite early, just after six because we were going on to my cousin's house for a bite and then watch a video. But I expect you know that as well.'

'I do, as a matter of fact. What was the video by the way?

'It was one of those early Terminator jobs, a bit far fetched if you ask me. Look, if this interview is going to get heavy, I'd like to have my solicitor here' added Vic, impatiently.

'It rather depends on you. No doubt you heard about the job. It was done by someone who was able to open three locks and a safe – a job that's got your hall marks all over it.'

'You flatter me, Buller, it sounds like somebody did a good job – a bit out of my league – any way Billy and me have had enough of prison. That last stretch, when we were stitched up by your mates was enough for a while.'

'Don't give me that shit, Steadman, what other kind of job could you do? The last honest one was when you were teenagers on your father's stall.'

'Now you're getting personal and, while we are on the subject, how far have you got with the investigation into our Dad's death, which wasn't an accident, as you well know.

'It's ongoing.'

'Who's dishing out the shit now? That's police speak for sod all. It looks as if Billy and me are going to have to do your job for you – you don't seem to be getting anywhere.'

'OK – OK' said Buller, realising he was getting nowhere 'Let's leave it there. I'll interview your brother and we'll check those alibis and get back to you.'

'Always a pleasure to do business with you, Mr. Buller' said Vic, leaving the room, satisfied that if there had been enough evidence against him, he would have been charged.

******

'Johnny! Johnny! Wake up, I've got to go to work, wake up.'

He could feel a light pressure on his shoulder as Tracey's voice penetrated his sleep-clouded brain. He wrinkled his brows and peered out of one eye. She was standing over him with a cup of coffee in one hand and the other on his shoulder.

'I must go to work now or I'll be late' she insisted 'will you be alright?' He opened the other eye. She was immaculate in her nursing sister's uniform, blue with white lace cuffs, with the broad belt with the large silver clasp accentuating her waistline. He could smell her freshness.

For a moment he thought that time had stood still. He had been awakened in this fashion countless times during their married life, especially when their shifts had clashed, or when he had been up half the night on CID work. Then they had been like ships passing in the night and it had placed an intolerable strain on their marriage. For her, being married to a CID officer was bad enough, with the awkward hours, cancelled leave days and messed-up meals; but the uncertainty was worse, the not knowing when he would return and whether he would be in one piece.

And when she was working shifts as well, it made the likelihood of the marriage succeeding a virtual impossibility.

The events of the previous twenty-four hours flooded back to him, his strapped ribs still hurt like hell and his aching wrists seemed to jolt his brain into gear. He managed a smile and replied 'Yes, yes, I'll be OK. Thanks for the coffee.'

'But how do you feel?' she persisted.

'A damn sight better than when I fell through your doorway last night - thanks to you' he added gratefully.

'Well I must go or I'll be late. You should find everything you need in the larder and fridge.'

'Thanks, love. Oh, there is just one thing.' His trained mind was already clear and working.

'What's that?'

'Don't alter your usual habits one bit. I mean don't load up with food or extra milk on the way home - just in case anyone is watching or quizzes the neighbours. I'll keep my head down. Just act naturally and we'll have a good chat tonight, OK?'

'Yes, alright' and, planting a kiss on his forehead, she said with feeling 'Welcome back, Detective Sergeant Johnny bloody Spencer.'

# CHAPTER SIXTEEN

'That's 'im now, the one on his own behind the two old gels' breathed Dave Wilson from the driving seat of the black Granada. The car was parked in the shadows under some overhanging trees on the opposite side of the road from 'The Sportsman'. The road surface gleamed brightly under the street lights after a shower which had fallen earlier. 'Drinking-up time' had long passed and the landlord was having his usual trouble persuading the customers to give him their glasses and go home. For some, the warm, friendly atmosphere of 'The Sportsman' was infinitely preferable to what awaited them at home, whether it was a cold, cheerless bedsit or a nagging wife and kids who should have been asleep and weren't. Whatever the reason, they were always reluctant to leave.

The other two occupants of the black car were Billy Steadman, whose huge frame filled the seat beside Dave in the front, and brother Vic, who was barely discernible in one corner of the deep back seat. 'Give him a minute and then follow' rasped the voice from the rear. Dave waited until Smithy, Johnny Spencer's snout, was well away from 'The Sportsman'.

'He'll either go to the chippy at the bottom of Stoat Street or straight home to his place at the far end of Buckmaster Road' said Dave, as he eased the car across the road to follow from a safe distance. He had obviously done his homework on Smithy's habits. However, his voice lacked enthusiasm. As his wife Dolly had feared, and had expressed forcibly at the old man's funeral, the brothers would expect Dave to help them establish themselves again. They needed wheels and he was the obvious choice. Besides, he owed them because it was their silence, after they had been caught for the job they had all pulled together, that had kept him out of prison. There was no way he could refuse, whatever Dolly said.

Unknown to the occupants of the car, a few seconds after they had pulled across the road to follow Smithy, a motor cyclist in black leathers and black helmet had emerged discreetly from the pitch black of an alleyway.

'He's heading for the chippy' commented Dave, as Smithy turned the corner into Stoat Street.

'There's too many people about, we'll take 'im after' ordered the voice from the rear.

'You know what to do, so no slip-ups' it continued menacingly 'Once he's in the back, I'll quieten the little bastard.'

They continued to follow at a safe distance, stopping every now and again as Smithy appeared to be in no hurry and certainly unaware he was being followed. Outside the chippy he stopped to light another cigarette. It was almost as if the fresh night air was affecting his lungs. He drew hard on the cigarette, coughed several times, spat in the gutter and entered the brilliantly-lit shop.

It was to be his first meal of the day. With only himself to look after, he didn't bother half the time – pub lunches and the chippy kept him going. 'Don't go much for that foreign muck, it's bad for you' he would wheeze, referring to hamburgers, kebabs, pizzas and the like.

Picking up the warm, neatly-wrapped parcel from the counter, he said goodnight to the owner and his wife and came out on to the street. Once there he decided to eat his meal right away, while it was still hot, rather than wait until he reached his flat. Flicking the half-smoked cigarette into the gutter, he watched it sizzle and go out.

Then, walking slowly towards home, he carefully opened the paper out to expose a liberal helping of crispy fish and golden chips, already well doused with salt and vinegar.

Engrossed in organising the meal in hand, he failed to notice the black Granada ease quietly in between some parked cars ahead of him and the lights go out. He had just sampled a piece of fish and a few chips with great relish when the car door suddenly opened in front of him. Then, blocking his view was the huge menacing frame of Billy Steadman. Panic and fear racked his body and brain; the moment he had dreaded since his meeting with Johnny Spencer weeks ago had arrived.

'But how?' his quick brain demanded. He had been most careful in leaking the information regarding the brothers. There was no way anyone could trace it to him.

It must be a try-on. Sweat broke out on his brow. Before he could utter a word, the rear door opened, Billy grabbed him and he was hurled into the back of the car. The fish, chips and paper flew into the air and scattered all over the car and pavement. The doors of the car slammed noisily and the tyres screamed as it sped away. There was hardly a sound from Smithy. It had been a slick, well-executed professional job and, obviously, not the first time that they had done it.

The brothers were well pleased with themselves, but the action had also been appreciated by someone else – the dark leather-clad motorcyclist. He immediately revved his engine, stamped one booted foot hard on the ground, spun the back of the bike round with a squeal and headed off at speed in the opposite direction.

Smithy found himself thrown violently into the back seat of the car against Vic Steadman, who wasted no time in pressing an evil-looking knife against his throat. 'Don't make a sound you little runt or I might just be tempted to stick you' hissed Vic, gleefully.

Smithy, in a panic, gasped 'Why? Why me? I've never done you no 'arm.'

'We just want to have a little word with you and, depending on your answers, will depend whether you do any more informing – snout!' he spat out the word 'Spencer's snout.'

'I don't know what you're on about' pleaded Smithy, beads of sweat breaking out on his brow.

'Just you think carefully, so that you can come up with the right answers when we get to where we're going.'

Smithy's mind raced, he had imagined many times that the day would come when the arrangement he had made with Spencer would come to this – but he had been so careful that there was no way they could trace things back to him. 'No' he assured himself 'they're just fishing. They must have suspected that Dace had something to do with their troubles since coming out of prison and they've picked on me because I'm the oldest and weakest. Well, I'll bloody well show them.'

After some ten minutes, Dave Wilson turned the car into a road which led to the side of the main railway line into London. Here many of the arches had been turned into garages and small businesses, some of them decidedly dodgy. Old Bobby Steadman used to keep his stall in one of the garages and the brothers had kept it on for reasons of their own.

Billy jumped out and unlocked the door. Returning to the car, he grabbed Smithy, yanked him out and threw him into the lock-up as if he was a rag doll. The dust of years rose as he hit the floor and crashed in to an old cycle, cutting his head on the pedals and causing blood to flow.

'Steady Billy, don't kill the little bastard before we've even started.'

'You said I would get my turn' insisted Billy.

'Yes, yes, but he's an old man and we've got plenty of time and remember – no-one will hear him, especially with the trains running overhead.'

Vic told Dave to park the car further away and keep watch on the lock-up to make sure that they would not be disturbed. He did as he was told, already regretting the fact that the information that he had volunteered had led to this situation. Knowing the Steadman's reputation for violence he knew that Smithy would be very lucky to come out of that lock-up alive.

Inside the garage, there were a number of strong hooks on the walls, which were used for hanging crates on. Billy had lifted Smithy and hooked him up on one of these, the hook going through the collar of his jacket. When Billy had done up the buttons at the front, this left him swinging with his feet barely touching the ground.

'Never thought I'd be using this old place again' commented Vic 'I'm glad we kept it on.'

Smithy, blood running from his wound into his eyes, realised that he would have to start talking soon, so he gabbled 'You called me a snout in the car – that's not true. I'm 77 years old – do you think I would have got away with it all these years without you lot finding out – you know everything that goes on – you would have found out.'

'The word is that you were Spencer's snout' insisted Vic.

'All I know about Spencer is that the law is looking for him and so are you – he's just disappeared.'

After a hardly perceptive nod from Vic, the first blow landed deep into Smithy's midriff, causing him to yell out in pain as all the wind was driven out of him.

'That's just for starters, you worm – now be sensible and tell us where Spencer is.'

'I've already told you, he's nothing to do with me' Smithy gasped.

The second blow was higher and to the left and there was a loud crack as one of his ribs took the full force. Billy was warming to his task; it was too simple, just like a punch-bag hanging on the wall. Smithy, on the other hand, was in real trouble, the pain was intense and he fought hard to contain it, wondering whether there was a slight chance that he could come out of this situation alive. This thought made him even more determined to withstand the pain as long as possible.

'Easy, Billy - easy. We want him to talk, remember.'

'He'll talk in a minute' snarled Billy, as he landed another blow to the other side of poor Smithy's chest, resulting in another loud crack, the sound muffled this time, as a train rumbled overhead on its way to central London. Smithy collapsed, his head dropped on to his chest and he lost consciousness.

'You daft bugger, Billy, how's he going to talk now? The poor sod's passed out' said Vic angrily.

'He's just trying it on, he'll come round in a minute' claimed Billy.

For once he was right, as Smithy gave a moan, opened his eyes and, summoning all his strength, he stared at the two brothers and said defiantly 'You two can go and fuck yourselves.'

This was too much for Billy and, ignoring Vic's pleas, he landed a blow directly to the heart which proved too much for Smithy to bear. This time it was for good. Smithy, through his defiance, had hastened his demise.

'Now look what you've done, you mad bugger, now we've got a corpse on our hands and we still don't know the answer.'

'Well, he asked for it, didn't he?'

'OK, Billy' said Vic resignedly 'Just go and get Dave and the car, will you.'

When Billy and Dave returned, they lifted Smithy down from the wall and, making sure no-one could see them, added a few kicks to the frail figure, before dumping him unceremoniously into the boot of the car.

They locked the garage and, back in the car once more, they drove away. Vic, who had been deep in thought, said 'Maybe we didn't get much out of the old bugger, but I've got a great idea of where we can dump the body.'

\*\*\*\*\*\*

Despite the fact that his house had been broken into and most of his silver stolen, Dace had a house full of guests and they were half-way through dinner in the large dining room, when he was disturbed by a ring on the door bell –

he answered the door and quickly ushered the latest arrival into the hallway.

'Honest Mr. Dace, I didn't know what to do, so I fort I'd better let you know quick like' panted the black-leathered motorcyclist, his helmet dangling awkwardly in his left hand. He was a pimply youth and his sweaty head, where the helmet had pressed the hair tightly down, looked almost too small for his body.

'Alright, alright, son' wheezed Dace 'but you should have stayed with them. Christ knows where they've taken 'im now.'

The youth looked incongruous standing there in his tattered old leathers amid the opulence of Dace's house. In fact, the surroundings were so overdone that the only thing that really fitted was Dace himself. Tall, ornate double doors with shiny brass fittings occupied most of one wall and he loved to sweep these doors open with a flourish to display a huge glittering chandelier which hung over an enormous dining table. Dace had always dreamed of owning a house and a room like this, after seeing one like it in the films. Only he had forgotten that, in the films, it was usually the butler who opened the doors to admit the guests. He cast an anxious glance towards the doors as if fearing that one of his guests would come out. Then he quickly dispatched the youth to check if the black Granada was parked outside the Steadmans' house. Ringing in his ears were also instructions to check the area and report back by telephone. That, at least, would give Dace time to think. The youth, pleased to be out of the house and back on his beloved motor cycle, departed as quickly as possible with a roar of the engine.

With trembling fingers and a worried frown on his face, Dace reached for a silver-topped decanter, poured himself a very large Scotch and collapsed into the nearest armchair. He had to think. 'Christ, it was getting close to home.' Smithy had been with him since the old days when they were both bookies' runners together. Only Dace had been more careful with his money. 'But why Smithy? He wouldn't hurt a fly.'

He racked his brain, tossed back the rest of the Scotch and automatically refilled the glass. Could the Steadmans have somehow connected the petrol bomb and the brakes on the van with him, and this was their way of letting him know? He shook his head, discounting the idea. Poxy had assured him there was no way that they could be linked with those incidents and Poxy was always right. It was Poxy who had arranged for the youth, who was a relative of his, to follow the Steadmans and he had done well, really - except he should have stayed with them. Poor Smithy could be anywhere now and he shivered at the thought of how the Steadmans were probably treating him.

He glanced anxiously again at the double doors, as sounds of laughter inside interrupted his thoughts. 'Poxy-yes, Poxy can deal with this. I must get back to my guests.'

He reached for the telephone handset, one of the old fashioned type, all brass and onyx, and dialled. He heaved a sigh of relief at the sound of Poxy's voice. A quick explanation followed and then, feeling much less worried, Dace put on a smile, opened the doors with his usual flourish and rejoined his guests.

## CHAPTER SEVENTEEN

Johnny was beginning to feel much more like his old self. His ribs still hurt and his wrists ached, but he had kept his head down and carried out Tracey's instructions to the letter. The long, lonely time between her leaving for work and returning had been an absolute bore. He longed to get back into action again. Whilst recovering, he had had plenty of time to think of Claire and the Steadman brothers and what his next move would be.

His enforced rest had given him plenty of time to ponder over his present situation. He went over and over in his mind his involvement with Claire and how he must have been responsible for the bomb attack on her flat. Then there was the appearance of her brothers and their insistence that he must have had his share of the £10,000 bribe which had landed them in prison. It just didn't make sense - Albert was as straight a copper as you are ever likely to meet. He recalled that one of the most successful cases they had dealt with together had been the kidnap of a young girl, the daughter of a wealthy banker. Along with many other officers, they had been involved from the start in most of the investigation, but together they had arrested the persons responsible. He remembered that on the return of the child to the distraught parents, the banker father, who had offered a £10,000 reward for the safe return of his child, had insisted that they should share the reward. Albert had explained that this was not possible and that he could donate the reward to the Police Widows and Orphans Fund. This had not satisfied the banker, who waited till his wife had taken the girl up to her room before saying to Albert 'Look, you and your partner took all the risks and brought the case to a successful conclusion. I can't tell you how grateful my wife and I are, and I would like to reward you both somehow. Is there any way that this could be done unofficially, no-one need ever know I assure you.'

Johnny could still hear Albert's response. 'That's very kind of you, sir, but it's just not possible - our jobs and pensions would be on the line. If you feel strongly about this, a mention of praise for the efforts of the police to the judge, when the case comes to court, would not go amiss.' There had been other occasions when money had been offered to them and they had refused. Albert was straight as a die, so why were the Steadman brothers still banging on about the alleged bribe.

Several days went by and, when he wasn't musing on the past, he began to feel better. To relieve the boredom, he started slowly to employ exercises he had used for fitness whilst in the Marines, naturally without the long arduous runs and forced marches - he still had to keep a low profile.

Fit or not, there came a point when he couldn't stand another day cooped up in the flat. Tracey had been an absolute brick and he felt guilty when he told her of his intention to move out.

'Where will you go?' she asked anxiously, adding 'I suppose it's no good me asking you what you intend to do, is it?'

'No love' replied Johnny, seriously 'Look, I'll never be able to thank you enough for all that you've done. You saved my life and I won't forget that, but I have to settle things.'

'Why don't you go to the police? Surely it's up to them now?'

'Yes, OK, maybe it is, but don't forget I started the whole thing and I can't tell them that, can I? I can't make a 'full confession', as the saying goes.' He smiled as he said it.

Tracey looked at him, saying 'You've used that word again.'

'Which word?'

'Confession. To you CID blokes it only has one meaning, hasn't it?'

'Well, yes' replied Johnny, not sure where the conversation was going, 'It's so much part of our job. Once you've caught the villain that's only half of it - you then have to prove it in Court. It makes life so much easier for all concerned if you can get a confession. But you know all this, what are you getting at?'

'Something you said the other night when we were discussing Albert and what he had said to his wife when he was in intensive care. Didn't the word 'confess' come into it?'

'Yes' he said.

'Well, the word 'confess' means only one thing to a policeman, but it means more to a Catholic.'

'But Bert wasn't a Catholic.'

'No, but maybe he was referring to a Catholic, going to confession, or even the confessional itself.'

He had spent hours trying to fathom out the meaning of Albert's message, without success.

'Did you have any dealings with Bert and the confessional?' Tracey persisted.

'No, of course not' Johnny laughed 'It was hardly a topic of CID conversation.'

'Wait though' he sat up, raising both hands, his face and eyes showing deep concentration. 'Bert and I did an observation once on a right villain from inside a disused church. It was a Catholic Church - something wrong with its foundations I think. We had to get special permission from the priest, I remember - he wasn't too keen on the idea, but we managed to convince him.'

'Go on' said Tracey 'and what did that have to do with the confessional?'

'Well, you know what an irreverent lot us coppers can be at times' Johnny paused, as if picturing the scene he was describing, 'The confession box was there in perfect condition and after we had completed the observation, for a bit of light relief, Bert sat in one side and I sat in the other.'

'Trust you lot - what happened then?' Tracey shook her head in mock disgust.

'Well, I confessed to Bert various sins I had committed with you the previous night - but I can't remember what they were' he added quickly.

'I can imagine' said Tracey 'and what did Bert say?'

'I shall always remember his plaintive voice telling me to say three 'Hail Marys' and put a pound in the poor box on the way out. To think he's no longer with us and I've had a right hammering. It must have been a judgement.' He shook his head slowly, his thoughts miles away.

'But do you think it could have anything to do with what Bert was trying to say?' persisted Tracey 'Up to now you haven't been able to come up with anything – have you?'

'No, you're right – it's a starting point, at least. Maybe he was trying to say 'confessional box' and couldn't get it out? But why? I don't even know if its still there. The church could be pulled down by now, but I'll certainly check it out' he added.

They settled to a hurriedly prepared meal with the last bottle of wine left over from Christmas. Nothing extra had been bought, as Johnny had instructed. By the end of the meal the bottle was empty, they were both merry and trying not to think about tomorrow, when Johnny would leave. Tracey had enjoyed having him at home with her, but with the Steadman affair still festering in the background, his presence was hardly a comforting one. In fact, the situation was still very much the same as it had been when they were married and he was in the CID, when uncertainty and danger were just beneath the surface. All the things that had contributed to the breakdown of their marriage were still there.

'It's time I moved on anyway' said Johnny jokingly 'the cupboard's bare, but I insist on replenishing it, so get set for the arrival of a food hamper from that famous store.'

'Don't be daft, I've quite enjoyed it and I've managed to lose a pound or two into the bargain. You know that old saying that "two can live as cheaply as one, if one doesn't eat anything" - well it works if one eats her meals at the hospital. I shan't be sorry to pack that in. I'd forgotten just how bad their meals were. Still, hopefully there's no harm done.'

They lazed together on the settee, with another drink, after clearing up. She was glad to relax after a hectic day, and he was pleased that he had made up his mind to move on and that he had already worked out his plan of action. He casually picked up a copy of the Evening Standard that Tracey had brought home with her and noticed a small headline 'Body of man found.' In his years in the police, and particularly the CID, he had read many such headlines, which were quite common in the great Metropolis. He read on.

**'The body of a man of about 70 was found today in the gardens of a block of flats in Brewster Gardens SW by the caretaker, Mr. P. Rogers.'**

Johnny froze. They were his flats! A feeling of fear and apprehension came over him as he read on.

**'Both arms had been broken and the features were so badly mutilated as to make identification difficult. Police scientists hope to identify the body through dental records, as there are no other distinguishing marks. House-to-house enquiries are being made and the police appealed to anyone who may have seen anything suspicious to come forward. Detective Inspector Buller is in charge of the case.'**

He couldn't believe his eyes. He read the article again.

'What's up, Johnny?' enquired Tracey, anxiously.

'Can you fix me another drink?'

Tracey left the room wondering what on earth was wrong.

The colour had drained from his face and he clenched his fists. His thoughts turned to Smithy, despite the fact that the body could have been of anyone - only the age was about the same. He convinced himself that it was probably the fact that the body had been found in the gardens of his flats that had him thinking this way - but it was bit of a coincidence just the same.

Tracey returned and handed Johnny his drink, which he sipped, deep in thought. 'Thanks, love' he said gratefully and, handing her the paper, pointed to the bottom of the page. 'Read that - it doesn't look too good.'

Tracey read the column twice. 'And you think that the body is Smithy, your old snout?'

'That's right.'

'But you can't be sure, that description could fit any old man.'

'It's the sort of thing that the Steadmans would do. I know the way their minds work.' He paused and then continued grimly 'If it is Smithy, it could be their way of letting me know that they have found out about the connection between us.'

'Then that means you're in even greater danger - you must go to the police.'

'I can't. That's the other bad news.'

'What do you mean?' asked Tracey.

'Of all the CID officers in the Met, the one in charge turns out to be that bastard Buller.'

'Oh, of course' cried Tracey 'I remember all the trouble with him before, when you were suspended. Didn't he report on you to that Board of Enquiry that you had to go on?'

'Yes - and he didn't do any of us any favours. He wasn't exactly over the moon when we were cleared either' added Johnny, despondently.

'So what are you going to do?'

'I don't know' he replied 'I'll sleep on it and let you know in the morning.'

# CHAPTER EIGHTEEN

The funeral of old Bobby Steadman was over, the bills had been taken care of by Claire, as her brothers were short of money, and she set about trying to pick up the threads of her life again. It was obvious that life could never be the same now that her father was dead and the brothers out of prison. The only reason for her remaining at home had been cruelly taken from her. Looking on the bright side, she was free; free at last to put as much distance between herself and her brothers as possible. Unknown to them, she had renewed the previously suspended application for herself and her father to emigrate to New Zealand - only this time it was for one only, and marked urgent. She had already contacted an aunt and uncle in Auckland and they had agreed to look after her until she settled and made a new life.

Meantime, the brothers had taken over the family home and Claire left them as much as possible to their own devices, staying at her own flat above the shop. She had told them that she had no intention of opening the florist shop again and lied convincingly about returning to secretarial work once more. Vic had demanded money for living expenses and Claire had given him enough to keep things ticking over smoothly, but she knew he'd be back for more. To her great relief, aided by the false set of accounts previously prepared, she had managed to convince her brothers that the business had not been very profitable. This had brought sneers of abuse from Vic who had always maintained that the money spent on her education was a waste. Now he had been proved correct, or so he thought.

Claire accepted the abuse and encouraged him to think that way. At the same time she discreetly visited her accountant and made arrangements for the preparation of the final accounts of her business for income tax purposes, for claiming the insurance from the fire and for the sale of the property. She set about systematically tying up all the loose ends so that, when the time came, she could disappear without a trace.

Making all these arrangements helped to occupy her mind and keep her sane. She missed her father terribly and, at the same time, her thoughts turned continually to Johnny. 'Where was he and what was he doing?' The last glimpse she had had of him, battered and bruised and leaning against the wall at the back of the florist shop, had remained with her and returned continually during her sleepless nights. 'Had he really only played her along in order to get at her brothers?' as Vic had cruelly suggested so many times. She was still confused. She had enjoyed his company more than anyone she had ever met and yet he had conveniently forgotten to tell her that he had once been a CID officer and, what is more, had been responsible for putting her brothers in prison. She was not too concerned about that, but 'Why hadn't he told her? Why? What reason could there be?'

She had asked herself these questions a hundred times and tried to recall conversations they had had to find some clue, but without success. All she knew was that, despite the mystery, she was worried about him and missed him. She felt that Johnny was not one to let her brothers treat him the way they had done and get away with it. So, perhaps, at the moment he was in hiding somewhere, recovering his strength and plotting revenge. This could only lead to more bloodshed and violence, something she abhorred.

Just at that time, Johnny was feeling liberated. To be in the fresh air again, after being cooped up, helped immensely and what pleased him even more was to find that the mews where he garaged his black cab was deserted. There was no question of him retrieving his old Rover from the underground car park at Hyde Park where Tracey had so cleverly hidden it. By this time it would have been checked out by the police and impounded. He backed the cab out of the garage, padlocked the doors behind him and drove cheerfully out of the mews. It was good to be behind the wheel again and for good measure, but also partly for disguise, he put on the old cloth cap and pulled it well down over his eyes. It was a slightly misty morning and the sun broke through to brighten up the day. He pulled out on to the main road to join London's bustling traffic. Keeping the 'For Hire' sign purposely unlit, he incurred the wrath of several people who were late for work or an appointment. Taking on a fare was the last thing on his mind as he steered the cab over Wandsworth Bridge and up into the Shepherd's Bush area. Eventually he was driving down a wide avenue with large Victorian houses on either side. After several hundred yards the avenue ran into a leafy square, at the far side of which was his destination. 'At least it's still standing' he remarked to himself. Seeing the huge, neglected Roman Catholic Church of the Virgin Mary, he pulled up outside, entered by a small side gate and made his way to a neat redbrick house which stood in one corner of the grounds. Pulling the old-fashioned bell he waited and found that he was in luck.

'Come away in, officer' was the cheerful greeting in Father O'Driscoll's broad Irish accent. This was followed quickly by 'Have you had an accident or something? Sure, you're not looking too well.' His eyes focusing on the marked face and bandaged wrists.

'That's right, Father' replied Johnny, adding cheerfully 'you know how it is.'

He intended his reply to leave poor Father O'Driscoll having to assume that the injuries had been received in the line of duty.

'You'll take a cup of tea with me, officer? I've just made a pot' said the priest, as he showed Johnny into a cluttered lounge full of knick-knacks acquired over many years.

'Yes please, Father, that would be most welcome.'

The priest was a short balding man in his sixties and inclined to waddle rather than walk and Johnny remembered how Albert had remarked on the fact after their previous visit. He waddled out into the kitchen and waddled back with a cup and saucer. Pouring out of a large brown pottery tea pot, he filled the cup and handed it to Johnny asking 'Would you like some breakfast – a piece of toast maybe?'

'No, no thank you, Father. It's very kind of you, but the tea will do just fine.'

The priest picked up his own cup and, settling back into his worn favourite armchair, paused and then announced 'They've solved the problem you know – sure they're going to underpin it with tons of concrete. My prayers have been answered.'

'Are they?' replied Johnny 'I'm pleased for you' wondering what on earth the old man was talking about.

'I don't know what I would have done if they had pulled it down. I love the old place.'

Johnny fell in at last – of course, the church – the reason why it was at present unused, something wrong with the foundations.

'Yes' the priest continued, in his lilting voice 'I didn't know that when your friend called the last time. He was most concerned.'

Johnny sat up quickly, almost spilling his tea. So Albert had been back.

'Can you remember when that was, Father?' said Johnny, trying desperately to speak in a calm voice, adding 'I was on another job so I couldn't be with him that time.'

'Yes, he said you were busy. It was just after Christmas a few years ago – I can't remember exactly which year - but I remember it well because he brought me a little present.' His watery grey eyes twinkled as he continued

'Something liquid to keep out the cold, you know – just for medicinal purposes.' He tapped the side of his nose with his index finger and gave a knowing look.

Johnny was just debating whether to tell the old priest of Albert's death when his thoughts were interrupted. 'I suppose you'll be wanting to check again, like your colleague did?' Johnny took the line of least resistance, rather than explain about Albert, and simply agreed, saying 'That's right, Father – if you don't mind, it's only a check, it shouldn't take long.'

So, Albert had gone into the church!

He continued 'We're pretty sure that the premises we had under observation are being used legitimately now.'

'Ah! Sure, I'm glad to hear that. By all means go and check and take as long as you like.'

'Thank you very much. I'll do it now, if you don't mind' said Johnny, keeping up the deception, but anxious to be on his own.

'I'm only pleased to be of help' the priest insisted, with a smile 'You boys do a wonderful job in these troubled times.' The word 'troubled' rolled off his tongue and Johnny had trouble himself keeping a straight face. He stood up, thanked the old priest warmly and headed for the church.

'So, Albert had been here without me' he repeated to himself 'but why – and why deceive the old Priest? He must have had a good reason.'

With mixed feelings he turned the black iron catch, pushed the heavy oak door open and entered the huge ornate cavernous church. He wasn't religious, but like most people recognised that for some a church was a very special place. His mind went back to a bright Sunday morning in Paris on his honeymoon, when Tracey and he had joined the other tourists and made the trek up to the Sacre Coeur. First the Metro, then through the narrow streets, small cafes and shops and the inevitable tourist shops full of knick-knacks and souvenirs. All the time climbing until eventually the Sacre Coeur appeared, white, shining and majestic on top of the hill.

The countless steps which, unless you took the funicular, had finally to be climbed, led on to a road which was full of Congolese selling silver, ivory and ebony souvenirs. Mounting the last few steps, they had finally entered the huge church to find it almost filled to capacity. Worshippers attending a service and tourists of all nationalities milling around the back and sides. People of all ages were lighting candles and then crossing themselves, after dipping their fingers in the holy water, and together with the pleasant musical intonations of the service, it had all provided one of those magical moments which had remained with him.

However, the scene confronting him now was quite different, silent, empty and dusty, with each sound or movement magnified a thousand times. He glanced around, stopping at the high, coloured windows behind the altar. It was through these windows that they had, with difficulty, obtained the evidence needed to put away two right villains. Such a good result that they had both received Commissioner's Commendations for their efforts.

Again his thoughts returned to Albert. 'Why had he come back?'

The job had been successfully concluded – there was no need. He found himself staring at the confessional situated to one side of the aisle. 'Confess' was what Albert had said. 'Could there be a connection?' He moved towards the wooden, highly-carved ornate structure as if drawn by some unseen force. He reached forward, swished aside the thick silk curtain and looked in.

Facing him was the seat and to the right the grill, through which the confession was heard. This was, in fact, the side which he had sat in and confessed jokingly to Albert seated in the other. He was no longer with us – maybe it was a judgement. He shook himself out of these thoughts, he didn't believe in all that stuff, anyway. All his police training and experience had taught him to deal in practicalities and hard evidence, not ideals or intangibles. He looked under the seat, around the walls and ceiling but saw nothing unusual. Then, moving next door, he repeated the exercise. Again there was nothing to provide him with the slightest clue, if indeed there was anything there to find.

'Oh well, it was only a long shot, an idea of Tracey's which was worth following up.' He stood staring at the confessional. 'But that doesn't alter the fact that Albert came back.' He repeated the last three words aloud. They echoed round the empty church and jerked him back to reality. 'Wait a bit though, there's a gap at the back. It doesn't fit flush to the wall.'

There was almost room to get an arm behind. He peered into the gloom but could see nothing. Still not satisfied, he slipped off his jacket, rolled up his shirt sleeves and felt right down both sides. Nothing. All he got for his pains was a dirty arm and shirt where the dust of years had been disturbed. Shrugging his shoulders, he rolled the sleeve down and replaced his jacket. It looked as if he had drawn a blank.

He sat down in a nearby pew to think. After several minutes of deliberation, his thoughts returned once more to the inescapable fact that Albert must have had a reason for coming back. The only place left was the open top, behind the ornate carving. But anything up there would have been visible to the balcony above, so that was unlikely. Feeling dejected he muttered 'I'd better check just the same, for my own peace of mind.'

He stood up and dragged the nearest pew over beside the confessional, hoping against hope that the old priest would not come in. As quickly as his damaged ribs would allow, he climbed up on the pew, grasped the carving for support and looked anxiously around the top. Nothing. Nothing but dust.

He was about to come down, convinced now that he had tried everything and that it was all a waste of time. He looked anxiously towards the side door, concerned not to offend the old priest, when he noticed that the dust had been disturbed at the far corner. He jumped down and dragged the pew further round towards that corner. Balancing again on the pew, he peered over the top. Two of the boards at that end appeared to have been disturbed. But surely that would have been visible from inside. Unless it was a false ceiling. He reached forward and with his finger nails managed to lift up the nearest board and then the second one came up easily. There, in the middle of the narrow space, was a brown paper parcel tied with string.

He couldn't believe his eyes and, with trembling fingers, he reached into the space and removed the package. It felt soft and was quite light. He placed it on the roof of the confessional to his left and replaced the two boards in their original positions. Lifting the package, he bent down and placed it on the pew.

Then he jumped down and, as quickly as possible, pulled the pew back into place again. He flopped down on the pew, staring at the package. Anxiously, unable to contain himself any longer, he grabbed the parcel and tore one end open to reveal its contents.

'Jesus Christ, it's money' he exclaimed, and the blasphemous words echoed eerily round the church. From what he could see, the parcel contained neatly arranged bundles of £10 notes and, counting one area quickly, he estimated that the package must contain about £10,000. £10,000! It was too much of a coincidence. What he had feared, but had been unwilling to accept, looked like being true. 'Albert had taken the £10,000 bribe!'

Good old dependable Albert, with whom he had worked on numerous occasions when there had been opportunities galore to accept bribes or make extra money.

The question had never arisen. There had never been the slightest reason to think that it might be possible. In fact, Albert, in view of his wife's commitment to the church and the assistance he had given there occasionally, had had to take considerable ribbing at times from his CID colleagues. Now, too many things that had come up recently added to Johnny's fears.

For one, the insistence of the Steadman brothers that they had accepted the money and that Johnny must have had his share. He pictured the hatred on Vic's face as he spat out the words in the basement of the florist shop, when he was being tortured. 'Don't give us that shit, Spencer - your mate had the money alright, all £10,000 of it and you must have got your share.'

Then, the priest's confirmation that Albert had returned to the church on a false pretext. And, finally, his dying words to his wife while he was in intensive care. It was all too much and it fitted all too neatly.

All except…Why? 'Why would he have done something which was so out of character? He must have had a good reason' Johnny told himself, still trying to find an excuse for his old colleague.

As he sat there alone in the huge church, the thought suddenly struck him. What the hell was he going to do with the money?

# CHAPTER NINETEEN

'We can't even bury poor old Smithy. They won't release the body till they've completed the post mortem and held an inquest.' It was an unusually worried Terry Dace speaking, although he was still behaving as expansively as ever, opening his hands out like a Jewish tailor. He continued 'He had no family to speak of, so I've told the police that I'll take care of everything – it's the least I can do.'

He had called a conference at his house, away from prying eyes and ears. It was quite normal for him to get his staff together at intervals, although today he was one short - the subject under discussion - Smithy the tic-tac man.

They were seated around the large table under the ornate glittering chandelier in his dining room, surrounded by all the rich trimmings which he loved so much. None of those present felt particularly comfortable with such a display of opulence. Each one believed that he could have found a much better use for the money which must have been spent to achieve such an effect. Each knew, equally, that they had no cause for complaint. All of them did very well out of Terry Dace's business interests.

The managers of his betting shops were present, as was the young motorcyclist who had reported the abduction of Smithy. Completing the picture were Dace's closest associates, Poxy Huston and the cool Tommy Stock. It was Tommy who replied to Dace's opening statement.

'That's fine, we all know that you'll take care of the money side of things, but what about those bastards the Steadmans - we can't let them get away with it.'

One of the hard-looking managers spoke up 'I agree with Tommy. They shouldn't get away with it, but we've got to be careful. The place is teeming with the law. What we've got to be sure of is that they don't connect any of us with the brakes on old man Steadman's van - or the petrol bomb.'

Dace interrupted forcibly. 'Alright. Alright. I agree with both of you, we've got to look after ourselves first. The last thing we want to do is to get carried away, do something stupid and drop ourselves in it.'

'So you're going to let them get away with it?'

It was Tommy Stock again, his steel-blue eyes menacing as usual between narrowed eyelids. 'Look' he continued 'I can take care of it in my own way, if none of you want to get mixed up in it.' He looked contemptuously at those seated around the table. 'It would be a pleasure, after what those murdering bastards did to old Smithy.'

Dace, red-faced and losing his temper rapidly, responded abruptly 'I'm sure you could, Tommy, no-one doubts that, but you've got to remember that Buller's in charge of this case. How long do you think it would take him to work out that you were involved in a solo hit job?' He paused for the message to sink in 'Think about that.'

'OK, OK' agreed Tommy, reluctantly, well aware of his reputation and very proud of it 'I admit that Buller's a smart bastard, but there's ways and means, you know.'

A spine-chilling look came over his face. He did not elaborate, but left each person present to contemplate what he had in mind. They squirmed in their seats, some lit cigarettes for something to do and all of them evaded those eyes. Finally Poxy, who refused to be intimidated, chirped up 'I agree with Terry – what's the hurry? Whatever we do it's not going to bring Smithy back and we can bide our time and sort them out later when things quieten down.'

Several heads nodded in agreement and one of the managers added 'Yes, and if this Buller's as good as you reckon he is, how long is it going to take him to work out that the Steadmans were responsible.'

'You're right' agreed Poxy 'the heat must be on them.' He paused and smiled 'After all, a hell of a lot has happened around here since they came out of the nick and the law must realise that.'

'You mean let the law take care of the Steadmans?' retorted Tommy, scornfully 'I'd rather do it myself.'

Dace called them to order, saying 'Look, the more I listen, the more I'm convinced that the best thing to do for now is nothing. Let's wait and see what happens. The Steadmans aren't going anywhere and they're not going to get away with what they did to Smithy, that I promise you - OK!' Those present sensed that the subject was closed and most of them nodded their heads in agreement, some more reluctantly than others. For the time being, even Tommy Stock agreed to sit back and await developments.

******

Later the same evening, not many miles away, in the front room of the Steadmans' family home, a similar meeting was taking place. The surroundings were neat, clean and old-fashioned and in complete contrast to those of the flashy bookmaker's house. The men sitting around the small table were, however, equally determined and voices were raised as each forcibly expressed his own opinion.

In the chair, conducting the proceedings, was Vic Steadman, and, as usual, on his right towered the huge frame of brother Billy. Still reluctant, but going along with the brothers, was the 'Wheels' man, Dave Wilson. His part in the torture and death of Smithy had sucked him back into the criminal ways that his voluble wife Dolly had predicted and feared. It was too late now, he could see no way of getting out and the terrible treatment meted out to Smithy was a timely reminder of what could happen to him if he crossed the Steadmans.

One other person completed the quorum. George Waites, whose pale-coloured face indicated to the initiated that he was an ex-con. Vic and Billy had looked after him whilst in prison and he 'owed them'. All favours outstanding were being called in for what was to be the final act.

They had tortured Smithy, but he had, in fact, told them very little. He had strenuously denied any connection with Johnny Spencer, more out of cussedness and hatred of the Steadmans than anything else. His weak frame and generally poor constitution had led to his losing consciousness rapidly before they had managed to get much out of him, and then he had never regained consciousness. Billy, angry once more at Vic's interference in what he considered to be his side of the business, had not helped by stamping on Smithy's face and frail arms, breaking both of them.

So the capture and torture of Smithy had been unsatisfactory, yielded nothing, and created further bitterness between the two brothers. They were still no further forward in their search for information. They had failed to establish a definite connection between Smithy and Johnny Spencer, and they didn't know who had been responsible for interfering with the brakes on their father's van and the petrol bomb attack. They argued vociferously, but the only thing they all agreed upon was that something had to be done to save face. Somebody had 'had them over' and, if they failed to mete out justice, then they could become a laughing stock in their own criminal world.

They had systematically considered a prepared list of possibles, mostly villains whom they had upset or had had to lean on at some time or other - even in prison. Anyone at all who had the slightest reason for not being pleased to see them back on the ground again. In the end, after several hours, the neat front room looked a mess. The atmosphere was stale, the table littered with empty bottles and beer cans, the ashtrays were overflowing and still there was no agreement between them. Eventually Vic called them to order announcing 'Look, we've considered everybody we can think of and the only definite connection is between old Smithy and Dace's mob. It's got to be them.'

'But remember, it was a connection between Spencer and Smithy that we were looking for' interrupted Dave Wilson.

'Yeah, you said you thought he was Spencer's snout, but he never admitted it, did he' snapped Billy, sulkily.

'Well, if you hadn't rubbed him out so quickly, maybe you would have found out' retaliated Wilson, his eyes glaring at Billy, who half stood up until Vic pulled him down, saying forcefully 'Cut that out, will you, we've got enough trouble without you two 'avin a go.'

Billy sat down reluctantly, shaking his brother's grip from his arm but still glaring in the direction of Wilson, who kept his eyes averted and looked straight into his beer.

Vic looked from one to the other and said angrily 'Use your bloody loaves will you and concentrate on what we are going to do about it.'

The fourth member, who had not been present during the abduction of Smithy, piped up 'I 'eard that Tommy Stock is the 'ard man of Dace's outfit. One of the cons was telling me that 'e's even done contract work. He's got to be somethin' special to do that and get away wiv it.'

Vic nodded 'That's right, I've heard that as well, but there's never been any proof. If it's true, then him and that Poxy Huston could have easily done the old man's brakes' he continued, nodding his head in agreement and seeming to think out loud 'They're certainly capable of doing it, and heaving a petrol bomb through a window doesn't take much brains or bottle, does it?'

'I've never liked that Tommy Stock' said Billy, quietly 'not since we had that run in with him at the dogs that time, when Dace was trying to fiddle the odds.'

'Yes' murmured Vic slowly, his eyes narrowing 'It's got to be them' he paused, and there was silence in the room as he announced 'I think the time has come for us to pay Mr. Terrance bloody Dace and his mates a little visit.'

# CHAPTER TWENTY

Dusk was fast approaching as Johnny parked the black cab and picked his way through a jumble of cardboard boxes and dustbins before he entered the open rear door of Sung's Chinese restaurant. The heat and smell of Chinese food and the sound of something crispy being fried greeted him, as did the owner Chin Sung.

'Allo meester Spencer – where you bin – why we don' see you no more?'

Chin was a short, fat, balding figure and he grinned toothily at the sight of Johnny.

He was wearing a white singlet, baggy trousers and a spotless white apron which was tied round his waist. He was as immaculate as his surroundings and never feared the visit of the local Health Inspector, unlike some of his

213

contemporaries. The sight of Chin in the kitchen meant that his wife and son were serving in the restaurant tonight.

'It's a long story, Chin' replied Johnny 'I'll tell you when I've got more time.'

'Meester Spencer – you in trouble?' queried Chin, his face and eyes showing concern 'Only we have that Meester Buller in here the other day and he say to phone him if you come here. I say I don' see you for ages.'

Chin had been in the country for nearly thirty years but his English hadn't improved much during the whole of that time. But he was always genuinely pleased to see Johnny, who had helped him with one or two problems when he first opened the restaurant. Not the least of these being a small-time villain and his accomplice who had tried to collect protection money. Chin had been grateful to Johnny for getting them off his back and they had been friends ever since.

'Chin, I'm starving. Could you fix me something, back here - out of sight?'

'Wid pleasure, Mr Spencer, jus' like old times, eh!' He grinned again, his eyes closing completely this time, as his sallow face wrinkled with pleasure. Johnny received a similar greeting from Chin's wife and Number One son when they came into the kitchen with orders for the restaurant. Soon he was tucking into a meal of clear soup, sweet and sour pork with rice and several delicacies specially prepared by Chin.

When these had been washed down with a couple of cold lagers, he felt much more human.

After their original meeting, Johnny and several of his CID colleagues had often frequented the restaurant, which seemed to stay open as long as there were customers, and this had proved useful on many occasions when they were working odd hours on observations and the police canteen had been closed. Now, Johnny and Chin chatted together between Chin's visits to the shining gas stoves to prepare dishes in odd-shaped pans, and Johnny told him as much as he felt was necessary to set his mind at rest.

'I also had those Steadmans here the other day, they try to get more money out of me, like before when you help me out' said Chin 'Luckily, Mr. Buller - he deal with them this time. But he still wan' to know if I know where you are.'

Johnny could well imagine how Buller would have applied pressure to find this out but, in order not to involve his Chinese friend any further at present, he said his goodbyes and disappeared the way he had arrived, through the back door.

Back in the cab once more, he was soon turning into the mews containing the garage. He was glad to find it deserted. If Buller was looking for him, then he would have no idea where he kept the cab and this could prove most useful, but he had to return to his flat sometime - he couldn't avoid Buller forever. The prospect of this meeting did not appeal to him one bit and he intended postponing the day as long as possible. Approaching the flat cautiously, he spent a considerable time sussing out the parked cars and likely observation posts, but he saw no one.

Unknown to Spencer, Buller's men had been keeping the flat under observation and they now immediately reported back to their boss at the station to the effect that Johnny had shown up. Buller got into his car immediately and drove towards the flat. As he did so he mused on the way in which their paths had crossed during their years of service.

It had started when they were both PCs in the same single men's section house in the West End, to which they had been allocated after training. Buller had more service and was already there when Spencer arrived. They had worked different shifts so, apart from seeing each other at meal times or in the TV room, nothing out of the ordinary had happened to cause the later animosity between them. Buller progressed through the ranks to the rank of Inspector and some years later found himself at the same station as Spencer. He had been assigned the job of reporting on Spencer to the Enquiry Board, in which he had kept the praise for his work to the minimum, but nevertheless was unable to ignore Spencer's Commissioner's Commendations. Despite Buller's promotions, what had happened years ago with a certain girl still rankled. He had never married and his present physical condition, overweight after years of CID work and his liking for a glass of lunch, had taken its toll. He wanted revenge of some sort on Spencer and was playing a waiting game.

Back in the early days as young constables, the situation had changed when they both turned up, with others from the section house, all spruced up, to a dance at the local hospital. Invitations turned up regularly and nurses and policemen, especially young ones, were often thrown together, possibly because they both worked shifts and served the community in all its horrific aspects. Spencer, Buller and the others entered the dance hall to find the nurses sitting all around the room, eager to dance, while most of the men headed for the bar in order to get dutch courage before venturing on to the dance floor. The evening progressed with Buller and Spencer taking a fancy to a strikingly good-looking girl called Caroline, who seemed more mature than her colleagues. She must have sent the patients' hearts racing when they had their pulses taken. One could imagine how she would look in her uniform with the belt and buckle showing off her figure, if the dress she was wearing at present was anything to go by. Buller was the first to invite her on to the floor, but Spencer claimed her for the next dance and so the evening progressed until it was time to go home. Both men had persuaded her to have a drink at the bar as they left the floor at the end of a dance. Each of them enjoyed the company of this bubbly, yet mature, woman and were eager to continue the friendship. Buller had managed to get her address and phone number and felt confident that he was ahead of Spencer but, when it came to the time for the last waltz and the question arose as to who was to take her back to the nurses' home, she had chosen Spencer, much to Buller's annoyance. The nurses had to be in at a certain time so there was no chance for Spencer and Caroline to get better acquainted. After a brief kiss goodnight, they arranged to meet the following week, when their shifts allowed.

Johnny returned to the Section House feeling elated and already looked forward to their next meeting – for Buller it was the opposite. They avoided each other as much as possible and, being on different shifts, this eased the situation somewhat.

Johnny met her the following week and on several other occasions, when they visited Thames-side pubs and went to the cinema and theatre. The friendship developed until, one fine evening, he suggested that a trip to Hampstead Heath might be a good idea. Caroline replied that she had a better one and, refusing to be drawn, took him to a very upmarket block of flats in the Earls Court area. Still keeping him in the dark, she rang for the lift which took them to the third floor, where she produced a bunch of keys and opened the door of one of the flats. After they got inside and closed the door, Johnny grabbed her, kissed her passionately and threatened her with a fate worse than death if she didn't tell him whose flat this was and what they were doing there.

'Come in properly and I'll explain' she laughed and, pulling away from him, entered the lounge and threw herself on to an enormous white leather couch. Johnny joined her, taking in the opulence of the room with its colourful abstract paintings on the walls, rich silk curtains at all the windows and an enormous TV in one corner. A floor-to-ceiling bookcase covered one wall and, between them and the TV, a large low table was covered with the latest magazines and art books. The floor was covered with the deepest shag pile he had ever walked on. To a young PC in a Section House, used to living in something similar to a horse-box, the whole place shouted serious money.

'Don't say a word' she said 'I was just as dumbstruck as you are when I came here first. Actually, my elder sister lives here. She had an Oxbridge education and married a much older merchant banker – this is just one of their places. At the moment they're in the Bahamas for a month and they have asked me to look in from time to time to make sure that everything is alright.' She paused 'Better than that, there's a single room which I can use any time I like' – she raised an eyebrow – 'I just thought you might be interested.'

'You dark horse' he said, grabbing her tightly 'You never mentioned this before.' She struggled in his arms, but unconvincingly.

'Maybe we should examine this room of yours to see if everything is in order?'

Johnny hardly had time to notice whether the room was as opulent as the lounge. He had eyes only for Caroline as they undressed each other. Her beautiful figure, which was good enough when clothed, was infinitely better naked. The nipples of her firm breasts already stood out in anticipation of what was to follow. She lay back on the bed opening her arms to welcome Johnny. He moved in slowly, there was no need to hurry especially as the owners were away for full month. He was no virgin, since his time in the Marines had taken him to many parts of the world and he had experienced many women. Now he just could not believe his luck.

Caroline was more than a willing partner and she wrapped herself around him tightly, as they kissed and fondled one another.

'So do you like my room, then?' she asked, biting his ear.

'It's alright, but I like the person that's in it better' and he gasped as her hand searched between his legs, rather more roughly than was necessary, he thought.

They made love tenderly and then roughly with such ease that Johnny's brain had time, during the ecstasy of the moment, to realise that Caroline was no virgin either. He then lost himself in the sheer pleasure as they moved in unison. They lay together exhausted, murmuring words of delight which made no sense – but it didn't matter. They visited the flat several times during the following month with an equally favourable outcome.

One day in the Section House, Johnny had bumped into Buller, who had looked at him with a cocky smile, quite out of character. This had made Johnny suspicious and he wondered whether Buller had ever managed to see Caroline after the night of the dance. And, one day, he said to Caroline 'I saw that bloody Buller the other day, remember him? He looked too pleased with himself for some reason.'

She hesitated, but then said that Buller had telephoned her many times and, to put an end to these many calls to the nurses' home, she had gone out with him. Johnny pressed her until she admitted that they too had been to bed.

However, as time went on, Buller had become a nuisance with his many calls and letters and, although she was sorry for him, she wanted to end the relationship. Buller wouldn't take her hints aimed at letting him down lightly and, in exasperation, she had finally told Buller that he, in no way, measured up to Spencer when it came to making love. That had been too much for Buller to accept and it had ended acrimoniously.

Johnny had found the fact that she had been to bed with Buller difficult to accept. She had pleaded that it meant nothing to her, but he was not convinced. Eventually their own relationship had suffered and then stopped when her sister and husband had returned and the flat was no longer available. It still rankled with Johnny that she had been two-timing him.

It was worse with Buller, who felt he had been humiliated. After his satisfaction at putting one over Spencer in managing to take Caroline out, it had all backfired on him, leaving him more bitter towards Spencer than ever. These reasons for hating him, and the possibility of getting his own back, went through Buller's mind as he approached the door of Spencer's flat and pressed the bell.

# CHAPTER TWENTY-ONE

Earlier, Johnny had entered the flats after glancing back to see if everything seemed quiet. He climbed the stairs as rapidly as his damaged ribs would allow, opened the door, and entered his flat. It smelt musty and unused. 'No wonder' he thought 'I've hardly been here.' He slipped off his jacket, which contained the money, and threw it over the end of the settee. After a quick look around, which showed everything to be in order, he headed for the drinks table where he found another bottle of the Scotch that he had brought back from Corfu. Corfu! God, so much had happened since his return that it seemed like years ago.

His fingers closed round the neck and his mind went back to the night when he had finished it - the night he had learned of Albert's death. Christ, that too seemed like years ago and the events of the past few days seemed totally unreal. He was jolted out of his thoughts by the sudden, loud, continuous ring of the doorbell. His thoughts raced 'Who the hell could that be? Was it a coincidence? Had he been followed?'

Looking at his watch, he saw that it was nearly midnight. The bell continued to ring. He crossed to the hall and looked through the spy hole. 'Shit' he exclaimed softly 'it's Buller. How the hell did he know I was back?'

Whoever had been keeping observation on the flat had done a good job - either that or he was slipping. Buller's voice boomed out officiously 'Don't mess me about. Come on, Spencer, I know you're in there.'

Johnny opened the door cautiously and replied bitterly 'I've got nothing to say to you, Buller.'

'Here or down at the station, it's all the same to me.'

Johnny shrugged his shoulders, pushed the door open, turned and made his way back into the lounge. He heard the door close noisily behind him, as Buller followed. He poured himself a large Scotch and sat down heavily on the settee beside his jacket.

'Oh God, he thought - the money' and he cursed himself for not hiding it as soon as he had entered the flat. He had been too confident that the flat was not under observation. 'Oh well, I'll just have to bluff it out' he told himself.

Buller's huge frame seemed to fill the armchair, as he settled opposite Johnny, and his heavy features conveyed pleasure as he taunted 'See you've been in an accident!' indicating the cuts and bruising on Johnny's face. 'Nothing too serious, I hope' he added, grinning.

'Nothing for you to concern yourself about, Buller' retorted Johnny, unmoved. The atmosphere was electric. They hated one another, these two, and it was almost as if hidden sparks passed between them. Buller spoke most officiously 'As you are no doubt aware, Spencer, I am conducting a murder enquiry.'

'Read about it in the papers' replied Johnny casually.

'Then you'll know that an old boy was found mutilated and murdered and dumped in the grounds of these flats. An odd coincidence, wouldn't you say?'

'Why odd?' queried Johnny 'It happens - and what's it got to do with me, anyway?'

'Well, after great difficulty the body was identified as one Smith.'

'Oh yes?'

'The buzz is that he used to be a snout' said Buller quietly.

'So what?' replied Johnny, trying to sound unconcerned.

Buller leant forward and, pointing a large fat finger at Johnny, spat out 'Your snout.'

'You're joking' replied Johnny, with mock amazement 'Anyway, I've left the job, remember, and you had quite a bit to do with my leaving' he added, with more than a touch of bitterness. There was no way that Buller could prove that Smithy had been his snout, because nobody else knew that he was - that was the value of a good snout. He knew this and so did Buller.

Buller fixed his eyes on Johnny and waited patiently.

'You've got the wrong man' said Johnny eventually 'Obviously, you've got your wires crossed somewhere.'

'I don't think so' retorted Buller 'But let's move on.'

As if the word suggested the deed, Buller heaved himself out of the armchair and started to pace the room. The combination of his huge overweight frame, coupled with the fact that he was slightly pigeon-toed, gave him a lumbering bear-like appearance. Johnny's eyes followed him back and forth, each time returning close to the jacket on the sofa containing the money. The pacing up and down was all part of Buller's interviewing technique, in the hope that in the end the accused would be partly mesmerised by the continuous movement. He would stop every now and again and then round on the unfortunate victim to demand the answer to a question, or to seek a reaction to a particular point. When he was satisfied with the answer, he would be off again.

Johnny had seen it all before and he remembered that his colleagues would joke between themselves that it was the only exercise Buller ever took, other than raising his elbow at the bar. Buller was disliked intensely by his colleagues because he was so ambitious, so pushy; the trouble was they also had to admit he got results, so at the same time they were extremely jealous. Johnny knew that he would have to really keep his wits about him if he was to survive Buller's questioning without giving anything away.

'I need a statement from you, Spencer, regarding your movements covering the period from before Smith's death until you walked in that door just now. Right!' He paused, as if to let his words sink in, and continued 'You've been missing from your usual haunts - I only hope you can provide an adequate explanation' he added sarcastically. He grinned and Johnny was amazed that he had never noticed before how bad his teeth were.

Johnny, who had no intention of letting Buller rile him, answered calmly 'Maybe I've got different haunts, as you put it, now that I'm not in the job!'

'Yes, maybe you have' suggested Buller, quietly but triumphantly, as it was the opening that he had been waiting for 'I wasn't surprised at all to hear that you had got shacked up with one of the Steadman family.'

'Sod the man, he has got to me' said Johnny to himself, as he felt his hackles rise. This was just the opening Buller had wanted.

Johnny recognised the tactics, remained silent, and fought to bring himself under control. Not wanting to let him off the hook, Buller pressed home his advantage and, emphasising each word, sneered 'I mean, they never did find the money the Steadmans paid you and your mate, did they?'

'Buller, you bastard, you know bloody well they tried to set Albert and me up' retorted Johnny angrily, adding 'You had enough to do with the investigation - you should know.'

'I do know' insisted Buller, his huge finger tapping his barrel chest 'and you can't deny being with the Steadman tart can you?' he taunted. Johnny controlled his desire to plant his fist on Buller's fat nose. He hated hearing Claire referred to in this manner, as if she was in the same category as her evil brothers, but he just had to swallow the taunts.

Buller was just trying to catch him off guard. He had stopped his pacing and stood over Johnny with both his hands gripping the back of the sofa. Recognising the signs of a breakthrough, he pressed harder. 'You can't deny that you were in bed with the girl at the same time as the petrol bomb went through the shop window underneath you. Now

Mr. Johnny bloody Spencer, you'd better start explaining to me quickly what all that was about.' His flushed face was only a matter of inches from Johnny's as he leant forward and spat the words out.

Johnny's brain was working overtime. 'I've got to give Buller something to get him off my back without incriminating myself.' Finally he said, in a controlled voice 'Look, Buller, I was only a humble sergeant, but it seems obvious to me that someone didn't like the idea of the Steadmans coming back on the patch again. Someone knew they were due out of prison the next day so they decided to get in first. It has to be something like that, the timing's too good.'

Buller nodded his head 'At last - at last you're beginning to talk like a copper. But who? Who hates the Steadmans that much?'

Johnny threw his hands wide and retorted impatiently 'I don't know, but surely with all your contacts you should be able to find out. That shouldn't be too difficult for a man of your calibre.' He pronounced the word in a facetious way, as if it were spelt 'cal-eye-ber', which prompted a quick reply from Buller.

'Don't give me that shit, Spencer, you know more about it than you're saying and, anyway, what about old man Steadman?' he added quietly.

'What about old man Steadman?' retorted Johnny quickly. Too quickly. He could have kicked himself. 'What was Buller up to?' His mind flashed back to Claire stumbling down the stairs into the basement where he had been tied up, to inform her brothers that their father had been involved in an accident. This time it was Buller's turn to remain silent.

Johnny tried to cover his confusion by casually offering 'He was involved in an accident, wasn't he?'

'Yes, a fatal one - and it wasn't a bloody accident.' Buller paused for effect, before announcing dramatically 'It was murder.'

Buller smiled again, satisfied that at last he had managed to get through Johnny's defences, as he could see that Johnny had not known of old man Steadman's death until now. Johnny racked his brains and cursed himself as he realised that Buller had got through. 'But what did he mean by old man Steadman being murdered. Claire had said nothing when she had freed him from the cellar, after she had returned presumably from the hospital. Had she known then?' He remembered that she had looked pretty upset, but he had been in such a state himself and so relieved to escape that he hadn't asked about the accident.

Buller had stopped pacing and was watching him closely. 'Bugger the man' thought Johnny 'he always was a good interrogator, one of the best.'

'You obviously didn't spend the last few days with the Steadmans then' gloated Buller and, rounding on Johnny, he demanded 'So where were you then?'

Johnny considered the question calmly. Tracey had done nothing wrong in harbouring him for a few days because, even though he was wanted by the police, she hadn't known that. 'As a matter of fact, I spent the time at my ex-wife's flat' he answered eventually.

'That's balls, Spencer, we had the place watched and there was no sign of you or anything out of the ordinary.'

'I can't help that, you must have sent some of your boys to do a man's job and they obviously didn't do it very well.'

'You mean you were too bloody crafty' proffered Buller.

'Suit yourself' smiled Johnny, for the first time since the interview began.

'Right, we'll check with your ex-wife. But I want a full statement from you, down at the nick tomorrow - 10 am - right?' Satisfied that he would not get much more out of Johnny that night, he had decided to finish the interview.

'OK, I'll be there' promised Johnny, relieved at the prospect of getting Buller out of the flat before he could discover the money.

'I expect you know the way' taunted Buller as he headed for the door, adding with a grin 'Don't worry, I'll see myself out.'

Johnny remained still until he heard the door close and was sure that Buller had gone. He relaxed for a few minutes and then rose, headed for the bottle of Scotch, and poured himself another large one. He felt the sweat run down his back as he threw his head back and downed the drink in one go. 'God, how I hate that man' he said, out loud, adding 'but at least he didn't find the money.'

He reproached himself again for being so careless, for not having hidden the money as soon as he entered the flat. He poured himself a final Scotch and carried it to the sofa. He would have to be much more careful in future. Buller was a crafty bastard and his timely appearance meant that the flat was under surveillance from somewhere that he had failed to notice. 'Oh well' he thought 'at least I'll have some protection for the night if the Steadmans are looking for me and I should get a good night's sleep.'

# CHAPTER TWENTY-TWO

Feeling much refreshed after a good night's sleep, a good shower and a change of clothing, Johnny made his way, the next morning, up the familiar steps of his old nick and reported to the Station Officer. It was a strange feeling, standing on the wrong side of the counter, after all the years of dealing with people from the other side.

The Station Officer, a round balding sergeant, greeted him cheerfully with 'Buller's expecting you, Johnny, make your way to the interview room' and added, with a broad grin 'You know the way, don't you?'

'There goes that great police sense of humour' thought Johnny 'I didn't realise how much I'd missed it.'

There can be no other organisation where the men take the mickey and play practical jokes with each other as much as they do in the police force. It has probably got something to do with the horrors of the job and the need to remain sane. Anyone too sensitive has to toughen up or they would soon go under. Indeed, anyone unable to stand the humour is reproached with the old Army saying 'If you can't take a joke, you shouldn't have joined.'

Johnny nodded, smiled back knowingly, and made his way down the corridor to the interview room. He had spent many gruelling hours in this room interrogating suspects and taking statements. If the interview was successful, the next stop was the charge room and finally the cells, followed by a Court appearance next morning.

Buller appeared, bluff and confident, accompanied by Detective Sergeant Charlie Read, one of Johnny's closest friends. Read looked awkward and acutely embarrassed at having to record Johnny's statement in response to Buller's questioning. They got straight down to business, with Johnny accounting for most of his movements satisfactorily, but conveniently missing out his clash with the Steadman brothers. He also insisted, despite fierce questioning by Buller, that he could throw no light on the persons responsible for the petrol bomb incident. He claimed, and Buller refused to accept, that his association with Claire Steadman was the result of a chance meeting. Buller said that he was just too old in the tooth to believe that. Unfortunately, Buller's mind continued to connect

Johnny and the Steadman family with the £10,000 bribe. He had been far from satisfied with the outcome of his enquiry at the time and, as Johnny was beginning to realise, his suspicions had been correct. He was a bloody good copper, was Buller.

Johnny, for his part, was certainly not going to enlighten him about his find in the church, or that his real connection with the Steadmans was one of revenge. The interview turned out to be a real cat and mouse affair, terminating with Buller announcing loudly 'Don't leave the country, Spencer, I shall no doubt want to see you again.'

Obviously he was far from satisfied with the statement and everything would be meticulously checked before he got back to Johnny again. Watching Buller's huge frame disappear through the door, Johnny heaved a sigh of relief. At least he had bought some time and could now operate in the open, with just the Steadmans to worry about.

Turning his attention to his old friend and colleague Charlie Read, who had stayed behind, he said cheerfully 'It's good to see you again, Charlie. Sorry to put you in such an awkward spot.' They shook hands firmly, the air of officialdom demanded by Buller no longer present.

'Where the hell have you been, you old sod?' queried Read 'Buller's been giving us hell for not finding you. He even accused us of not trying too hard.'

'I realise it must have put you all in a spot, but it would take too long to explain and, really, the less you know at this stage the better.'

'That's all very well' he replied seriously 'but you look as if you could do with some help.' He paused, looking anxiously at Johnny's face, and continued 'Look, I know you wouldn't tell Buller, but who did mark your face?'

'I can't tell you now, Charlie, but I will. Look, all I need is just a little more time to sort things out and then I might be able to do you all some good. Just keep Buller happy and listen - I may want to get a message to you without him knowing, OK?'

'How do you propose to do that?' queried Charlie.

Johnny thought for a moment and then said 'I know, check twice a day with Chin at the restaurant, right?'

Read nodded and, as they were leaving the room, gave his old colleague a knowing look and fired a parting shot 'Alright Johnny, play it your way, but mind how you go with those Steadmans - they don't mess about you know.'

Johnny filled his lungs and breathed deeply on reaching the street. The ordeal hadn't turned out too badly after all, which made him even more suspicious because it was out of character for Buller. He turned left and walked briskly towards the first corner where he turned, stopped and remained out of sight for about thirty seconds before retracing his steps.

On reaching the station entrance, he was almost knocked over by the hurried exit of two young detective constables stumbling down the stairs, obviously detailed by Buller to follow him. Their confusion and embarrassment was plain to see.

Johnny grinned at them. He was beginning to enjoy himself, and it wasn't over yet - now he had to lose them completely. He did this without much difficulty and, feeling sorry for the young lads, who would get a roasting from Buller, he made his way to the mews to collect his cab. Wearing sunglasses and with the old cap pulled well down at the front, he looked like any one of hundreds of other taxi drivers.

He headed for Claire's flat, feeling that he had to see her again not only to satisfy himself that she was alright, but also to find out about the death of her father. He dare not go near the Steadmans' family house and had to assume that Claire would eventually return to her own flat. He just couldn't imagine her living at the old house and looking after the brothers she hated.

With the black cab parked under some trees a discreet distance from the flat, he settled himself down and prepared for a long wait. He noticed that the front of the florist shop, including the front door, was boarded up completely and this meant that he had to watch only the mews entrance. On the front of the shop he noticed a 'Sold' notice stuck over an 'Under Offer' sign, so obviously Claire had decided to cut her losses and sell up. 'But where would she go? Had she left already?' These thoughts, along with the memory of the good times that they had spent together, milled around in his head as he waited. It was mid-morning. He thought that she might have gone shopping. The curtains at the window of the flat were apart but whether they had been drawn earlier or not, he had no way of knowing.

He waited for the rest of the morning and passed the time filling in a crossword.

Then it was nearly 1 o'clock, as his stomach had told him several times and as his watch confirmed. He had just started to consider the safest place to get some food when the familiar figure of Claire, carrying a shopping bag, appeared at the end of the street. With a sigh of relief, he started the engine, slipped into first gear and moved towards her, drawing level just as she was about to turn into the mews. The sight of the black cab must have registered with her because she hesitated and looked searchingly at the driver. 'Can I drop you somewhere, lady?' piped up Johnny, cheerfully.

The look on Claire's face was a mixture of surprise and anger 'Where the hell have you been, Johnny Spencer? Why haven't you been in touch? I've been worried sick' she blurted out, the words tumbling one over the top of the other.

'Get in the cab, love, and I'll answer your questions' said Johnny, looking around anxiously. Tears welled in her eyes as she did as ordered and entered the cab. He set the meter running and made sure the 'For Hire' light was out; the last thing he wanted was some nosey young copper stopping him for a breach of the Cab Regulations. Once out of the street he turned, pulled back the sliding window and enquired over his shoulder 'Are you alright? I couldn't contact you – I'll explain later.'

She leant forward in her seat to be nearer to him and answered 'Yes - yes, I'm alright now, but it's been hectic' adding anxiously 'But what about you? The last time I saw you, you looked terrible.'

'I'm OK now. Look, I'll explain everything when we get somewhere quiet, alright?'

'OK' she answered, sitting back again in the spacious seat of the cab.

As he drove eastwards through the bustling lunchtime crowds, her eyes lingered on the back of his head, his neck and his shoulders and she remembered the night she had run her fingers through his hair and dug her finger nails into his well-muscled back as they had made love. Her face changed as her thoughts hardened when she recalled what had happened next - the petrol bomb and all hell breaking loose; the faces of her brothers taunting her that Johnny was the detective sergeant who had put them in prison and that he was just making a fool of her to get back at them. She shook her head unbelievingly. They were an evil pair of bastards and surely Johnny would explain. As if on cue, he drew up and parked the cab.

She had been too busy with her thoughts to notice that the cab had been climbing for the past few minutes and that now they were in Greenwich Park, high above the Thames close to the old Observatory. Johnny had taken tourists here many times and it seemed to him an ideal place to mingle with the crowd and not be noticed.

The tourists certainly were out in force. There were Americans, Japanese and, as the cab doors were opened, he caught the sound of French being spoken. Cameras clicked noisily as people had their photographs taken outside the world-famous dome of the Observatory or around the corner with one foot either side of the 'Meridian Line'.

Johnny helped Claire down from the cab and for a moment they held each other close. He enjoyed the contact, the familiar smell of her perfume and the freshness of her hair filled his nostrils. Still with some doubts in her mind, she broke the contact first, thinking that there were still too many questions to be answered.

'Let's go somewhere quiet where we can talk' she blurted out. Her voice was stern and determined, as if she had rehearsed many times what she would say when they next met. 'Alright' replied Johnny, and taking her by the arm he steered her silently along the tree-lined walk. The view, unnoticed by them on this occasion, was one of the most beautiful in the whole of London. Below them spread the magnificent Royal Naval College, neat and pristine against the rich green of well-manicured lawns. Beyond that, the Thames curled round the Isle of Dogs past Greenwich Pier, where the pleasure boats, full of yet more tourists, disgorged their passengers under the towering masts of the famous Cutty Sark. The shining river then headed north before turning once more to enter the City of London past St. Catherine's Dock and Tower Bridge.

They came to an empty park bench on which Claire sat down quickly and, as Johnny joined her, she burst into the rest of her prepared speech 'I have to know the truth, Johnny. My brothers tell me that you are a detective sergeant and that you were responsible for their last spell in prison.' He started to interrupt, but Claire insisted firmly 'No wait, let me finish. I'm sure they deserved to go to prison, that doesn't come into it, but what does concern me is that you never once mentioned the fact that you were in the police.' She drew a deep breath and continued 'You must have known all the time who I was, despite the fact that I never told you.' She was white-faced and trembling now and her voice faltered 'I enjoyed our friendship so much, but you used me. Why? Oh, but why?' She was pleading now, her eyes full of tears as she searched his solemn face.

He reached forward and took both of her hands in his. The moment he knew he would have to face, ever since he had planned revenge and started the whole deception, and which he had been dreading, had arrived. He held her hands tightly and she made no attempt to withdraw them. Looking into her eyes, still moist from her outburst, he started to explain firmly but tenderly 'I can tell you almost everything and I'll explain at the end why it has to be so.' He then related the whole story of his suspension because of her brothers' allegations of bribery, of his appearance in front of the Corruption Enquiry Board and his reasons for leaving the police. He continued with the death of his Inspector friend, Albert, and his vow to discover the truth. Looking into her dark eyes, he continued seriously 'I admit that the day I came into the florist shop I was looking for Claire Steadman - I was grasping at straws. I had no idea what I intended to do, but I had to make a start somewhere.'

He tightened his grip on her hands and said 'What happened next when we became friends and enjoyed each other's company was not by design - it happened naturally.'

'But you could have told me' she insisted, unconvinced by his argument. Her eyes welled up again with tears 'You must have realised that I'm not in the same category as my brothers, or presumably you would have stopped prior to us going to bed together. Or was that all part of the plan too?' she added bitterly, withdrawing her hands suddenly.

'Look Claire, all I can say is that I have dreaded the day, the moment, this moment, when I would have to tell you the truth.'

'Yes, but you still haven't told me all the truth have you?' she flashed 'I've had plenty of time to think lately and all I know is that since I met you the following things have happened in my life.' She counted out on her fingers. 'One, my father died in suspicious circumstances. Two, my shop is destroyed by a petrol bomb. Three, my brothers come out of prison and already the police are interviewing them about the murder of some old man – they've even been asking me to account for their movements. As if I care about what they do.' She turned and faced him, with tears streaming down her face, and sobbed 'My whole world has fallen apart since I met you. I don't know what to believe, I'm so confused.'

Johnny tried to take her in his arms to comfort her but she shrugged him off. 'What else could he say? He daren't tell her the truth - the fact that he had set the whole series of events going.' In the end, he simply confirmed his previous explanation by saying briefly 'I understand why you feel like this, but I can only ask you to trust me. One day, perhaps I'll be able to tell you the full story.'

She stood up quickly, wiped her red-rimmed eyes with a handkerchief taken from her handbag, looked straight at him and said firmly, in a voice now very much under control 'I'm sorry too, Johnny, because I'm just not satisfied with that answer.'

She turned on her heel and started to walk away. He caught her arm and pleaded 'Please don't let it end like this. Claire, come on, let me take you home.'

She went with him back to the cab and climbed in without saying a word.

Once in the cab he headed quickly for her flat and, as he drove, he racked his brains, without success, to think of some way to give her the explanation which she required. The journey was completed in silence, each engrossed in private thoughts.

Soon the cab was entering the road which led to the mews and, when it stopped at the entrance, she jumped out quickly before he could leave the driver's seat. Slamming her door, she said briefly 'Don't concern yourself with any explanation, I shan't be around much longer to hear it anyway. I've made all the arrangements to emigrate to New Zealand and I fly out next week.'

As she turned to go, Johnny pleaded urgently 'Claire - please - wait – listen' and he jumped down from the cab and came quickly round to the front 'Please let me see you off, at least.'

She hesitated, thought for a moment, and finally said 'Alright, but I'll make my own way there, so don't offer. Heathrow 10 o'clock next Tuesday morning!' As she turned without a backward glance and disappeared into the mews, the words 'I'll be there' rang in her ears.

# CHAPTER TWENTY-THREE

The Coroner had decided at the inquest on poor Smithy, the tic-tac man, that his heart had stopped as a result of the dreadful injuries he had received from persons unknown and excessive smoking; no doubt due to the 'roll-ups' he much preferred to the 'tailor-mades' which, he maintained, '…were a bleedin' waste of money.'

It was now to be the day of his real cockney funeral.

Wreaths started to appear and were placed carefully on the pavement outside Dace's extravagant house in the beautiful tree-lined road.

A van with a catering logo on its side drew up and three men began unloading pots, pans and cold-boxes and, welcomed by Dace, they entered the house. This was not to be a 'sausage and sandwich' funeral reception, since

Terrance Dace had his reputation to think of and, besides, it would be a good chance to show off his beautiful house. Smithy, after all, had been one of his 'boys' and would get an appropriate send-off.

Dace's two minders, the evil Tommy Stock, appropriately dressed in black, and Poxy Huston, were the next to arrive, followed closely by the managers of his betting shops and their wives - the shops had closed for the day as a mark of respect. They added their wreaths to those on the pavement before entering the house for a pre-funeral drink. Dace, who had come out to welcome them, was very extravagantly dressed and, with the ever-present cigar either gripped between his teeth or in his podgy hand, he waved to illustrate some point or other.

As the sun crept over the treetops to brighten the scene, the sound of horses' hooves could be heard ringing out. Approaching the house was a shiny funeral coach drawn by two high-stepping jet-black horses with head cockades, which nodded up and down as they trotted. They were beautifully groomed and inside the silken interior of their coach was a coffin, on top of which was a wreath of pure white flowers which spelt out the word 'Smithy'. Finally, at the end of the coffin, were two white gloves, one crossing the other - the tools of the trade of the tic-tac man. No more would they signal, with great dexterity, the odds in the main ring to Dace's stall in the popular ring.

As the hearse pulled up outside the house, the funeral director and several assistants appeared from one of the following cars. They started loading the wreaths into the hearse until the inside was a blaze of colour, and the remainder were carried to the waiting cars.

By this time, a considerable crowd of neighbours and sympathisers had gathered.

Smithy, the loner, may not have had any relations, but he certainly had many friends. It would take the group a mere fifteen minutes to walk to the nearby crematorium.

At 10.30 am Dace appeared, followed by Stock and Poxy and the betting shop managers with their wives. They lined up in that order behind the hearse and, with the funeral director ahead and with the hearse and the rest of the sympathisers bringing up the rear, they made their way slowly on foot to the crematorium.

This would be the farthest that Dace had walked in years and his overweight body waddled between his two henchmen. People lined the route and Dace nodded to acquaintances, as he proudly displayed his wealth and respect for Smithy, who had worked for him for many years.

After the short service in the chapel, the wreaths were laid out in the Garden of Remembrance. Later they would be sent to the nearest nursing home and Dace's name would be prominently displayed.

## CHAPTER TWENTY-FOUR

Johnny lay in bed in his flat, in that blissful state of being half-asleep and half-awake, when suddenly he was jerked rudely into consciousness by the shrill note of his telephone.  Sitting up, wrinkling his still-closed eyes and annoyed at being disturbed, he fumbled for the bedside lamp switch. Squinting through half-open lids, he saw that it was 7 am.

'Who the hell was ringing him at this time of the morning?' He made his way, yawning and scratching, to the phone in the hall. 'I must get an extension to the bedside' he thought, as he picked up the phone and gave the number in a not too friendly voice.

'That Mr. Spencer?'

'Who is this?' replied Johnny firmly.

'A friend, Mr. Spencer. Just a friend. I've got some information that I'm sure you'll be interested in.' The voice, unfamiliar to Johnny, sounded fairly young, with a London accent. It was edgy and nervous.

'Oh yes' replied Johnny casually, having had this kind of conversation many times during his CID career. He added 'I'm no longer in the police.'

'I know. I know that' agreed the voice urgently 'it's to do with things what 'ave 'appened to you lately. Can we make a meet?'

'Look, I don't know who you are' insisted Johnny 'and how do I know you're not setting me up for something?'

'Honest, it's straight up, Mr. Spencer, but I can't say much over the blower. Look, if I was to say that I was a friend of old Smithy's, poor old sod, would that 'elp?' The voice was pleading now and Johnny realised that he would get no more over the phone, so after thinking for a few moments he agreed 'OK, where shall we meet?'

'You pick the place, Mr. Spencer' urged the voice, anxious to please now that Johnny had agreed.

'Can you get to the multi-storey car park in Croydon by 8.30 this morning? The main one at the Whitgift Centre?'

'Yes. I'll be there.'

'You come up to the top floor on your own, by the lift - understood?' ordered Johnny, adding 'I'm only waiting ten minutes, mind.'

'Right Mr. Spencer, don't worry I'll be there' repeated the voice and rang off.

Johnny replaced the phone slowly, deep in thought 'Could this be a set-up by the Steadmans or could his luck have changed at last? It was about bloody time. Nothing seemed to have gone right lately.'

The voice had sounded genuine - genuinely frightened, not just nervous, but as if working under pressure. His judgement had always been pretty good in the past, he argued to himself 'Yes, he would take a chance - nothing ventured etc.' Despite being fully awake now with the adrenalin flowing, he managed to snatch a few more hours sleep. He had almost completely recovered from his injuries and felt stronger every day. After a shower, he dressed leisurely and consumed a spartan breakfast, promising himself that he would take time out to stock the fridge with food.

Just before 8.15 am he was in the cab and approaching Croydon. He remembered with sadness the day, which now seemed ages ago, when he had collected old Smithy and taken him south to Chipstead Valley Road and, there in the cab, had put his plan to him. Neither of them had known that it would set in motion a chain of events which included meeting Claire, resuming a relationship with his ex-wife, two deaths, the burning of the florist shop and his own torture at the hands of the Steadmans. Perhaps it was fate that had led him again to Croydon, a respectable middle-class area, rarely associated with crime and criminals, unlike some of the neighbouring boroughs a few miles north. Perhaps it was here that he was to meet someone who would help bring the disastrous events to some kind of conclusion. If that was at all possible. Always the supreme optimist, he felt that it might happen.

He joined the queue for the multi-storey car park along with the commuters and early shoppers. He climbed quickly to the roof level, an easy task with the versatile steering lock of the cab, and parked on the roof directly opposite the down exit. As he had anticipated, the floor below was still empty, so that if anyone suspicious did drive up to the roof, he could still get away. He left the cab quickly and checked out the top lift exit which was one floor down - it was clear. He returned to the roof level and for a moment looked over the parapet and across Croydon. It was going to be a fine day, the sun was trying to break through light cloud. Below him he could hear the noise of the grinding traffic as it fought its way north towards London. Although the car park was fairly high, it was surrounded by skyscraper office blocks which towered above him. The place he had chosen for his secret meeting was, in fact, in clear view of thousands of people at their desks, if they chose to look out of their windows.

He returned to the cab, started the engine and kept it running. He checked his watch - it was 8.25 am - and kept his eyes on the car ramp from the lower floor. At 8.30 am, on the dot, the figure of a young man, well-built with dark hair and wearing a black bomber jacket and jeans, emerged on the ramp. His eyes swept the whole floor in one movement; then, satisfied that it was clear, he made his way further up the ramp towards the roof. Johnny watched him approach, and thought that something about him was vaguely familiar - then he recognised him. His heart jumped and the reaction must have caused him to rev the engine. It was Dave Wilson, a small-time villain who used to run with the Steadmans. Wilson must have heard the engine rev and sensed Johnny's fear, because he waved quickly in recognition, taking care to keep his hands clear and well away from his body.

Approaching the cab he chirped up 'Hello Mr. Spencer - no sweat – I'm on my own.'

Johnny, who could see that no one was following him, replied 'You're Dave Wilson, aren't you?'

'That's right.'

'But you're one of Steadman's mob.'

Johnny's voice must have frightened him because he stammered hurriedly 'I was, I mean, I am - but I want out and I can't get out.'

Johnny was familiar with this predicament, having come across it many times before. Looking at Wilson's worried face, he could see that it was a classic case of someone being sucked in and, if it was by the Steadman gang, then no wonder he looked worried. He had no chance of getting out.

'Jump in the cab' nodded Johnny, switching the engine off. He turned, opened the sliding window and, when Wilson was settled and the door closed, demanded 'So what's it all about then, Wilson. The Steadman's would kill you if they saw you talking to me.'

'I know - I know that, Mr. Spencer' the words came spluttering out 'but I've got to get out somehow. They're fuckin' mad those Steadmans and I don't want to end up going away for years.'

Johnny looked at him. His anguished face showed lines beyond his years and his soft watery eyes were red-rimmed with huge bags under them, no doubt caused by lack of sleep. His hands trembled as he lit a cigarette to calm his nerves. The enormity of what he was about to do seized him and he collapsed into a fit of coughing. It was almost as if some force was trying to prevent him from saying what he was about to say. He drew hard on the cigarette again, this time his lungs accepted the smoke and he exhaled, feeling comforted.

Johnny had waited patiently, not wishing to rush him, but finally he said 'Come on, Wilson, let's get on with it, I haven't got all day. What have you got for me that's so important?'

Wilson swallowed hard, his eyes moved from side to side as if checking finally that they were alone, and he blurted out 'There's going to be a carve up. The Steadmans, me and another geezer are going to take care of Dace's mob.'

'Oh yes' replied Johnny, as casually as possible 'so why should that bother me? None of them are particular friends of mine.'

Wilson persisted 'I 'eard that the brothers had given you a goin' over and I thought you'd want to get your own back, like.'

'But I'm not in the Force anymore, so why should I be interested?'

'Maybe you're not in the Force, Mr. Spencer, but your mates still are. Detective Sergeants Read and Johnson - and Buller' he added.

Johnny smiled at the suggestion that Buller was a mate of his 'You seem to have done your homework well' praised Johnny, nodding his head, and then he asked 'Are we about to get to the real reason for you telling me all this?' Wilson coughed again, shifted uncomfortably on the seat and replied 'I've done a lot of thinking lately and the only thing that I can come up with is – is…' he hesitated, the perspiration running down his anguished face '…is perhaps I could be left out of the frame when it all happens…' then, as if to excuse himself, he added quickly '…I'm only driving, anyway.'

He looked anxiously at Johnny to see his reaction, relieved that everything was now out in the open. 'Right' thought Johnny, his face impassive 'now we know the score.'

'You know I can't promise you that' he replied, adding 'even if I was still in the job.'

'No, but you could fix it with your mates' Wilson insisted.

'Please, Mr. Spencer' he pleaded 'it's my only chance. My wife has threatened to leave me and the kids, if I go away again. Look, I'm not a real villain, Mr. Spencer, you know that.'

'I can't promise anything, you know that, but I could put in a good word, it might help.'

'If you could do that, Mr. Spencer, I'll take a chance - at least it's something.' He leaned back into the deep upholstery of the back of the cab for the first time during the meeting. After a few seconds he reached for another cigarette, pressed it on the end of the butt in his hand and puffed hard.

Johnny waited again, knowing that Wilson was gathering himself to give the final details; the procedure always followed the same pattern, he had seen it many times before. The sweat ran down Wilson's nose and gathered at the tip and he brushed it away angrily with the back of his hand.

'It's Thursday night - at Wimbledon Dog Track - in the car park after the last race.'

The words came rushing out and Johnny could smell the mixture of fear and sweat coming from the man whose face was shiny and flushed. The deep vertical line had appeared again as his eyebrows wrinkled and came together. He drew hard on the cigarette, his hands shaking so much that the ash spilled down onto his trousers but he made no attempt to brush it off. For the second time he relaxed, relieved it was done and now there was no going back. He pulled out a grubby handkerchief and mopped his face.

'Phew, it's 'ot in 'ere, can I open the window?'

'Go ahead' replied Johnny and watched as, with shaking hands, Wilson wound down the cab window and took the opportunity to gulp in a few mouthfuls of fresh air.

'Any mention of shooters?' asked Johnny quickly.

'No, Mr. Spencer, there was no word of them at all' he confirmed eagerly.

'Knives?' persisted Johnny.

'Well, that Vic, he 'as a bit of a reputation wiv one, but you know that!'

'Yes' replied Johnny 'I do know that! Anything else you want to tell me?'

'No, Mr. Spencer, that's all. Do what you can for me, will yer' he pleaded 'they'd kill me if they found out.'

'Alright I will, but remember I can't promise anything.'

'Yes, OK, Mr. Spencer, thanks' he reached for the door handle and had the door half open when Johnny stopped him.

'Just a minute, you said you were only driving. Is it your own car?'

'Yes, I've been driving the Steadmans ever since they came out. Why?'

'Well, it might help to change the number plates on the night, but don't let anybody know - understood?'

'Yes - yes - thanks again, Mr. Spencer' he shot out of the cab and headed quickly for the lift. On reaching to ground floor he made his way into the Whitgift Centre and entered the nearest café. It would have to be tea to calm his nerves until he could get something stronger.

Johnny, meanwhile, got out of the cab, opened both rear windows to let in the fresh air and then made his way down the ramps. Pausing only to pay the minimum charge, he turned northwards and headed for his flat. Suddenly unable to control his emotions, he thumped the steering wheel with elation. The meeting with Wilson had been more successful that he had dared to hope. 'At last! - At last!' he shouted out loud, oblivious to the strange looks from the other drivers around him 'Something's going my way.'

On the way home, he called at the Chinese restaurant and left a cryptic message with Chin for his CID mates. It read 'Trouble - stand by for late Thursday evening - come well prepared – don't inform Buller - he will be engaged elsewhere.' He chuckled to himself as he read the message through. If all went well, Buller would end up with egg all over his face.

The question of the £10,000 had nagged at Johnny ever since he had discovered the package hidden in the roof of the confessional. Time and time again he had cast his mind back to events just prior to the Steadmans' allegation, when he and Bert had worked so successfully together. There seemed to be no reason - no set of circumstances that Johnny could imagine - why Bert Thompson would have accepted that money. If it had been anyone else, maybe he wouldn't have been so certain. Yet there was no mistaking the fact that the money was there and Bert's dying words had led him to it - so he must have taken it. In the end his CID training and knowledge of human nature forced him to reduce this problem to basics. It had to be one of two possibilities - Albert, unknown to him, must have had either a mental problem or a physical problem. The first he discounted. Mentally he had always been sharp and well-balanced, right through to the night of Johnny's farewell do, when he had pleaded with him not to leave the Force. Physically? Well, he had always seemed OK. He'd been down in the dumps and depressed whilst suspended, but that was understandable - he remembered how low he had felt himself at times. He made up his mind there was only one sure way to find out and that was to call on Bert's doctor.

# CHAPTER TWENTY-FIVE

Johnny had phoned from the Chinese restaurant and, fortunately, Dr. Robertson agreed to see him after his morning surgery. The doctor, who was also the Divisional Police Surgeon, was well known to Johnny as they had worked together many times. The cases varied from GBH, when the Doctor had mainly stitched up the unfortunate victim, to murder, when he was the first medical person called to the scene and required to pronounce life extinct.

Entering the surgery after a short wait, Johnny was welcomed cheerfully by the large red-headed Scot. His strong handshake reminded Johnny that, although his rugby playing days were over, the doctor still kept himself in good condition. The old photographs of his student hospital rugby team and his county, could be seen amongst the usual certificates of competence to practice medicine.

'You're not looking too good, Mr. Spencer, that cut should have had some stitches' he boomed 'Obviously the cab driving is not agreeing with you.' The Edinburgh accent was still very much discernible. His remarks were made in a joking fashion but Johnny's unusual gait and the marks on his face had not gone unnoticed.

'It's more than I can say for you, Doctor' replied Johnny, managing a smile 'you look disgustingly healthy.'

'Well, I try to keep in shape, as you know. We must have another game of squash sometime.'

'Yes - yes, that would be good' replied Johnny and he winced as a pain shot through his ribs, consciously reminding him of the lie.

'Now, seriously Mr. Spencer' the doctor continued, as he settled back in his huge leather-back swivel chair 'How has life been since leaving the Force?'

'I've had my ups and downs' replied Johnny 'and it hasn't been easy, but it's early days yet.'

The doctor nodded and waited, his red bushy eyebrows raised, sensing that the pleasantries were over and that at any moment the reason for the visit would be revealed.

'Actually, it's not me that I've come about' Johnny half-blurted out 'It's about Albert Thompson.'

'A great shame - and a good friend of yours' the doctor's voice lowered, his words sincere 'I'm sure you miss him. But how can I help?' he queried, spreading his huge hands.

Johnny drew a deep breath. He had thought hard about the best way to introduce his subject to the doctor. 'I can't tell you the full story – you'll have to trust me, Doctor.' He struggled with the words, his eyes pleading 'I've got myself involved in something which indirectly could have been caused by an inconsistency on the part of my old colleague Thompson.' He felt his temperature rise and he was sure his face had reddened as beads of perspiration appeared on his forehead.

Dr. Robertson brought his huge hands together in front of him, each finger and thumb touching its opposite. 'Take it easy, Mr. Spencer - relax!' he examined the shape he had made with his fingers and continued 'Just tell me as much as you feel you can - I understand' he added comfortingly.

'Doctor, I really need to know about Albert's state of health around December about four years ago.'

The huge Scot continued to examine his hands 'About the time you were both suspended and appearing before the Corruption Board?' he queried astutely.

'Yes - yes, that's right' agreed Johnny, thankful that everything was now out in the open.

'Normally, of course, it would be out of the question for me to give you information about a patient, but as poor Mr. Thompson is no longer a patient of mine then I can't see any harm, if it will help?'

'It will - and it is necessary, I assure you' urged Johnny.

'I still have his notes on file' he buzzed his receptionist and asked for the notes.

'Although' he continued 'I can tell you most of the details from memory. As he was a police officer, I took a special interest in the case.'

'Fine. Then what I really want to know is whether he had any worries that he kept to himself - I mean healthwise?'

'As a matter of fact, he did have some worries' replied the Doctor quietly 'In fact, there was a time when your friend was convinced that he had cancer.'

Johnny was astonished. He mumbled 'He didn't say anything to me about that.'

'Perhaps not, but apparently both his mother and father died of cancer when they were quite young and he wanted his fears kept secret so as not to cause any further worry to his wife and family. I arranged for him to have the necessary tests.'

'And?' demanded Johnny, anxiously.

'They proved negative in the case of cancer, but what they did show was that he had an ulcer, no doubt caused by all the worry - an occupational hazard in your job, as you well know' he said, spreading the huge hands again.

'So what happened?'

'I treated him successfully with tablets, but it was a heart attack that killed him.'

Johnny shook his head and muttered 'I'm amazed. He kept a thing like that from me and I worked with him every day.'

The conversation was interrupted by a knock at the door and the receptionist entered and placed a neat folder, containing the medical notes, in front of the Doctor. He pulled the notes out, glanced at the last page, looked up and said slowly 'I take it the fact that he was worried about having cancer could have a bearing on the reason for you being here?'

'Right in one, Doctor' replied Johnny 'You've been around police a long time and it shows. But what I really want to know is the actual date he came to see you convinced that he had cancer.'

'That's easy' replied the doctor, looking through the notes 'he came to see me on December the 10th. I wrote a letter for the hospital the same day and he took it with him to make an appointment. It's all recorded here.'

Johnny felt as if a terrific weight had been suddenly lifted from him because, although this latest discovery did not excuse his friend's action in taking the money, it did make it a lot easier to bear. OK, he himself had suffered, as well, with the accusations levelled at him - and not without reason as it now turned out. Bert must have been desperate and worried out of his mind to have made a deal with the Steadmans. It could only have been to provide for his wife and family after his death. Obviously he had died of the heart attack before he could use it, or maybe having taken the money he had just left it where it was when he found that he did not have cancer after all. Perhaps he had given his wife the message when he thought he was dying, to enable Johnny to clear his own name. Whatever the reason, it made no difference now.

His thoughts were interrupted by the doctor repeating 'I said I hope that the information solves your problem.'

'Yes - yes. Sorry, Doctor, I was miles away' Johnny apologised awkwardly, adding 'Thank you again for being so understanding. Perhaps one day I'll be able to tell you the full story.'

'Yes, I would like that' replied the Doctor 'I'm only too pleased to have been of assistance. Let me know how the cabbying goes and don't forget that game of squash.' He rose and extended the huge fist again and Johnny winced as he shook it.

'Thanks again for all your help, Doctor' said Johnny, as he made his way out of the surgery door and then into his cab.

He sat motionless in the driver's seat for some time, turning over in his mind the fresh information which had come to light. He had the answer now, but he still had the problem of what the hell he was going to do with the money.

# CHAPTER TWENTY-SIX

It was late afternoon on Thursday. Johnny stretched a handkerchief tightly over the mouthpiece in one of the local phone boxes. Keeping the conversation as brief as possible, in case a check on the call was being made, he summoned up his best cockney accent to inform Buller that 'Spencer's up to somefink tonight and he needs watching.' The act must have been pretty convincing because it fooled Buller - no mean achievement.

Much later, under the cover of darkness, Johnny left his flat and made his way nonchalantly down the stairs. Pausing at the entrance to the flats, he checked the time on his watch - it was 9.30 pm - and at the same time he glanced along the row of vehicles parked down the street. Thirty yards away someone was watching from a car. It had to be Buller. He made his way unhurriedly on foot towards Clapham South Underground station.

Someone was tailing him. He smiled to himself and muttered 'Right, Mister bloody Buller, now we begin the run-around, and am I going to enjoy this.'

Pausing to buy an evening paper, he was able to check in the reflection of a window that his tail was still there. It was - and it was definitely Buller. He bought a ticket and made his way through the barrier and on to the escalator. It was a strange feeling making the long journey down into the bowels of the earth and wanting desperately to know if Buller was still with him, but not daring to turn around. The station was relatively deserted. The rush hour had been over for some time now and the evening theatre and cinema goers would be in their seats enjoying the performance. Not many people were travelling northwards and that suited his purpose fine.

After a short wait, he boarded a Charing Cross train and sat down on one of the seats facing the centre of the carriage. He noticed Buller enter the next carriage just before the doors closed and stand with his back towards him. Johnny relaxed behind the Evening Standard, fairly confident that Buller knew his destination. He would have thrust his warrant card in the face of the man in the ticket office and demanded to know this. He wouldn't have taken the man's word, however, he would have to stay with him and check his presence at each station to be sure he didn't lose him. Johnny smiled to himself, recalling that the scene he was about to play was very much like the one in the film 'The French Connection' which took place on the New York Subway. The main difference, however, was that in this case, although giving the impression that he was trying to lose his tail, in fact it was the last thing he wanted. He was relying on Buller's egotistical opinion of himself to keep on his tail. He would never imagine that Johnny would string him along to this extent. Despite thinking like this, Johnny racked his brains to consider ways of making the act convincing. At each station Buller half-turned to check that Johnny was still in his seat, the task being made relatively simple as there were few passengers.

When the train reached Embankment, Johnny rose and, as soon as the doors opened, got out and made his way along the platform towards the stairs which led to the Circle Line. In order to do this he had to pass Buller, who had to remain on the train to avoid a confrontation. Opposite the door where Buller was standing, Johnny stopped as if to check his route on one of the large Underground maps on the wall. 'I might as well make life a little difficult for him' he chuckled to himself, as he slowly traced his finger over the map. He could imagine Buller getting in a flap as time was running out before the doors would close.

Buller was trapped. There was no time for him to make it to the other exit further down the carriage. He was stuck and he would be in a right panic.

Johnny waited until he heard the hiss of the doors and their rumble as they started to close before slowly moving off. He heard the doors almost close and then angrily break open again as something prevented them from closing completely. He imagined this something being one of Buller's large feet but he didn't turn round.

He chuckled again as he followed the yellow signs leading to the Circle Line.

He was enjoying himself so much that he even threw some small change in the direction of a pair of scruffy student buskers, whose music filled the long, glazed tunnel. The long-haired youth strumming a guitar nodded his thanks and his flute-playing girl companion signalled her appreciation with her eyes and Johnny took the opportunity to check that Buller was still in tow - he was.

At the Circle Line platform the procedure was reversed, Buller having to jump on the train several carriages down, just as the doors were closing, to make sure that Johnny did not leave the train at the last moment. Johnny smiled to himself and then self-consciously checked that none of the passengers were watching him. He wondered if Buller had seen 'The French Connection' and decided that it was highly unlikely. He couldn't imagine Buller as a film buff and he was never at home enough to have seen it on the television.

At this moment, Buller must have been wondering what the hell was going on because Johnny's ticket was for Baker Street and the Circle Line was not the most direct route. His plan depended on timing and he had allowed an average of two minutes per station for his leisurely trip clockwise around the Circle Line. The journey passed without incident and, on reaching Baker Street, he made his way quickly to the surface and out of the station.

After the comparative calm of the Underground, he found the Marylebone Road noisy and busy with traffic as usual. The many taxis drifting around, killing time until the theatres emptied, reminded him that he should have been out earning. He sighed at the thought. When all this business was over, hopefully he would be free to carry on with the new life he had chosen. Up to now he had only just got started and he grudgingly reminded himself that he had hardly made enough so far to cover the cost of the road tax and insurance.

He shook off the mood, quickened his step and headed eastwards past the now deserted Madame Tussaud's. During the day tourists from all over the world would be clamouring to visit one of London's most popular attractions. Johnny turned left into York Gate and past York Terrace whose majestic houses looked out over

Regents Park. Crossing the Outer Circle, he made his way quickly to the Inner Circle and Queen Mary's Rose Garden, which was an absolute picture with every conceivable rose in full bloom.

He checked his watch again and nodded with satisfaction - the timing was just about right; up Broad Walk and he would reach his destination. Another five minutes should take care of it. Turning left, he joined the Outer Circle again outside the Zoological Gardens, still on the tourist trail. Being a Londoner, he had visited the Zoo at various stages in his life from infancy through school days, and even the odd occasion as an adult, and it still held a certain fascination for him. Some of the animals, restless in their cages and not yet settled down for the night, could be heard baying and growling.

He checked the time again, crossed to a phone box on the other side of the road and, taking the opportunity to confirm that Buller was still with him, he made the all-important telephone call to the CID room at his old Station. This time there was no question of him covering the mouthpiece; this time there was no reason to fool anybody.

He had achieved what he had set out to do, namely to get Buller well away from South London at this particular moment and, just as important, to provide himself with an alibi at the same time.

He strolled casually back across to the entrance to the Zoo. He could just see Buller watching him from cover some 50 yards away. He looked through the deserted turnstiles and happy memories flooded back to him of whole days spent here with school friends and relatives. As he turned to go, he looked at the glass-covered notice boards which displayed prices of admission. 'Blimey, they've gone up a bit since I was here last' he thought. The boards also displayed details of some of the attractions within. One item in particular caught his eye. With a chuckle to himself he took from an inside pocket his Parker felt-tip pen and making sure that Buller could see clearly he boldly circled one word 'Monkey'. Then he turned away quickly, regretting only that he would not be able to see Buller's reaction when he saw what he had done.

# CHAPTER TWENTY-SEVEN

The car carrying the Steadman brothers and George Waites, and driven to Wimbledon by Dave Wilson, eased its way quietly into the car park of the dog track and stopped in the shadows. This in itself was unusual, as the last race was just about to start. Punters who wished to avoid the departing crowds, and those who had lost enough money already, were long gone.

It was a clear, warm night and the bustle of the crowd could easily be heard, accentuated by the cries of the odds offered by the bookmakers. The air was heavy with the smell of onions from the hot dog stands, mixed with cigarette and cigar smoke, which billowed out like clouds under the bright lights surrounding the track.

Inside the car the atmosphere was tense and no one spoke, other than to remark about the lack of freshness of one of the passengers whose fear could be smelt. Vic Steadman, his face lined and his lips pressed together tightly, had gone over the plan many times, until he was satisfied that each person knew exactly what he had to do. A roar from the crowd reached their ears as the last race began, and the dogs leapt from their traps yelping and straining in pursuit of the hare. As it was the last race, the encouragement from the punters was particularly vociferous - the empty beer cans and whisky bottles no doubt had something to do with that. The noise reached a crescendo as the dogs crossed the line and died away almost as quickly as the handlers collected their dogs and led them away.

There were the usual expressions of disgust from the losers as their betting cards were torn and thrown to the ground to join the others forming a multi-coloured carpet. At the same time, excuses, explanations and recriminations could be heard, such as 'he was in the wrong trap' or 'that was a fix, he could have won by a mile' or 'if only the three dog hadn't interfered with the two dog on the first bend ...'

'If only ...' - it was always the same old story.

The lucky few who had won headed for the Tote or the bookmakers to collect their winnings, happy no doubt to finish the evening on a lucky streak. The majority, though, streamed out of the stadium and headed for home, or perhaps to the pub for a pint before closing time.

For Terry Dace and Poxy Huston it had been a good evening and, with the favourite unplaced in the last race, there was very little to pay out. They were soon packed up and heading for the stadium bar to join Tommy Stock for a quick drink before leaving. There was no need for Dace to run a stand at the dogs really, because his betting shops ensured a very good living for him and all his staff. However, for Dace to give up the dogs would be like trying to break the habit of a lifetime, since it was his whole life. He enjoyed the atmosphere of the betting scene, the bustle and noise, the smells and the challenge, such as it was. He knew only too well, that nine times out of ten he would come out on the right side. He and his companions were one of the last groups to leave the bar and the staff were waiting to close. Having said their goodbyes, they headed for the car park, voluble and in a cheerful mood.

Approaching his car, Dace extracted a huge cigar from a leather case, peeled off the band and reached into a pocket of his waistcoat for his silver clippers. Having trimmed off the end, he lit the cigar and puffed hard as he settled himself into the rear seat of his old Daimler. Tommy Stock moved in beside him while Poxy, one of the few he allowed to drive the car, took the driver's seat. The powerful engine sprang into life and ticked over quietly.

Dace relaxed and puffed on his cigar as the car eased forward through an almost deserted car park. The only movement came from a hot dog stall trundling along ahead of them and now approaching the narrow exit. The car headlights picked up the gaily-painted stall and the white-coated figure bent almost double towing it.

'It's old Limpy Jones' remarked Poxy 'he's a bit late getting away.'

'Yes, mind you don't knock the poor bugger over' added Tommy Stock sarcastically, as he was not one of the drivers that Dace trusted with the car. 'Hang about' he added anxiously 'something's not right.'

His experience of being in tight situations where his life sometimes depended on it had alerted his brain.

'Something's not right' he repeated, as his drink-befuddled brain struggled desperately to work out what wasn't right. As the car drew almost level with the stall he realised too late just what wasn't right.

Limpy Jones wasn't limping.

Before he could react, the stall swung across the front of the Daimler causing Poxy to slam on the brakes violently, cursing as he did so. The car skidded forward on the loose gravel raising great dust clouds as it came to rest only inches away from the stall. Inside the car there was confusion, as Tommy Stock was thrown forward, his attempted warning lost as he struck the back of the front passenger seat violently, forcing the air from his lungs with a horrible curse. He struggled to regain his position from the floor behind the front seat, fully aware now that it was a situation of danger. But he was too late. Before he could recover, the door on his side was wrenched open to reveal the figure in the white coat.

He had been right - it wasn't Limpy Jones.

It was an evil Vic Steadman, whose piercing eyes had an almost inhuman look. The realisation was of little consolation to Tommy Stock, as the knife in Vic's hand streaked towards him. Panic and the will to survive gripped him as he jerked himself backwards, but the glistening knife followed, entering the soft area above his collar bone and continuing into his neck and throat. The terrible scream which came from his mouth ended suddenly, stopped by the blood released into his wind pipe as the knife point plunged deeper.

Dace, who had also been thrown forward, was struggling desperately to get up from the floor when the writhing body of Tommy Stock, spewing blood everywhere, landed heavily beside him. Vic withdrew the knife triumphantly and an indescribable animal-like noise escaped through his bared teeth, which glowed white in the semi-darkness of the car - he had achieved the most important part of the operation.

Tommy Stock, the hard man, was out of action and now the rest should be easy. However, he had underestimated Poxy Huston, who was sitting in the driver's seat fully aware of what had just happened behind him. Activated more by fear and the desire to survive than anything else, he slammed the car into reverse, causing a scream of complaint from the gearbox. He saw Billy Steadman's huge frame heading for his door. It was a situation he had been in before and he knew the best way to deal with it. His right hand slipped down quickly and released the door catch and, just as Billy was reaching to open it, he crashed the door open with all his strength. The edge of the heavy door smashed into Billy's groin with a sickening thud. A yell escaped from his lips, which was a mixture of surprise and pain, and he seemed to remain motionless, suspended in the air until, like an action replay, he dropped slowly, writhing and cursing, to the ground.

Poxy, still aware of Vic's presence behind him, didn't wait to see the results of his action. Letting out the clutch with a jerk, he pressed hard on the accelerator and with a roar the car responded and flew backwards. This action threw Vic Steadman off balance, just as he was moving towards Dace with the knife and, with a curse, he struggled to hang on, half-in and half-out of the car.

Dace, meanwhile, having recovered from the initial shock of finding Tommy Stock's body slumped across him, spurting blood all over him and the leather seats of his beloved Daimler, saw the opportunity to strike back. Heaving Tommy Stock off, he leant over his lifeless body and viciously crushed the burning end of his fat cigar on the back of the hand that Vic Steadman was hanging on with. With a scream of pain, Vic disappeared from view as the car continued backwards, causing the third of his henchmen George Waites, whose job was to deal with Dace, to leap for his life.

Vic Steadman's carefully laid plans were going awry.

Poxy slammed on the brakes, crashed the gear lever desperately into first gear and spun the steering wheel, letting out the clutch as he did so. The spinning car wheels screamed and tore into the loose asphalt, sending dark showers into the air, until at last they gripped and the car leapt forward towards Billy. He was dazed, bleeding and in considerable pain and getting to his feet when the Daimler hit him. The sickening sound of bone being smashed could clearly be heard mingled with Billy's screams as he was knocked backwards to the ground again. The car lurched violently, as first the heavy front and then the rear wheels jerked over his body, crushing his pelvis and both of his legs.

His screams were drowned by the roar of the engine, usually so quiet, as Poxy, seeing a real chance of escape, stepped on the accelerator and sped towards the exit.

The clouds of dust and asphalt settled finally to reveal the crumpled, lifeless body of Billy Steadman. The well-muscled frame, of which he was so proud and which he had worked so hard to shape and mould whilst in prison, was unrecognisable on the churned-up ground. Vic had scrambled to his feet comparatively unhurt and had seen the car run over his brother and had heard his awful screams.

'Billy!' he yelled agonisingly 'Billy!' and scrambled towards him, for once showing genuine concern for his brother, but no sound or movement came from the crumpled mass. 'God, that bastard Dace will pay for this' he spat out the words as he reached the motionless figure. He looked around him quickly, fully aware that his plans had gone terribly wrong and his natural instincts for survival screamed at him to escape - to run - to leave the scene as quickly as possible. But he must get Billy to hospital first - Dace could wait.

He turned and yelled desperately, in the direction of the Granada parked in the shadows, for Dave Wilson to come and pick them up. Wilson, who already had the engine running, had watched the whole fiasco, glad that he was only along as the driver. Now he slammed the car urgently into gear and started to move towards them.

Vic, meanwhile, had been joined by George Waites, who counted himself extremely lucky not to have been involved so far, but who was now anxious to help. Vic grabbed his brother's arm and shouted to Waites 'Give me a hand to sit him up.'

'You can't move him, Vic, you'll kill him, he's in a bad way.'

'We can't leave him here' snapped Vic, panic showing in his eyes for the first time 'we've got to get him to hospital – he'll be alright in the back of the Granada.' He looked anxiously again for the car. Before the argument could proceed any further, or any more harm could come to Billy, the problem was solved. The sound of sirens and police cars arriving reached their ears. Two cars screamed into the car park and forced the escaping Daimler to a halt. A third car disgorged uniformed officers in all directions.

Dave Wilson, who had been uncertain what he should do as he drove the Granada across the car park towards the others, suddenly made his mind up 'It's now or never!' Accelerating quickly, he squeezed the black Granada between the first exit and the hot dog stand with inches to spare and was gone. As he sped from the scene Vic's voice could be heard uttering oaths and promises of retribution above the roar of the engine.

To Dave's surprise, his many anxious glances in the mirror showed no-one following him. Vic stood cursing him and promising himself that Dave, too, would regret the day he ran out on Vic Steadman.

Vic's first instinct had been to make a run for it, but the odds were too great and then there was Billy. Despite the image of a man without feelings, which he had always felt he had to maintain, there had always existed a strong bond between the two brothers. Since childhood Billy, the younger, had always looked after his physically less adequate brother but, as they grew up, Vic's superior brain and ruthlessness had made Billy obey him without question. Now, as he was led away by Johnny Spencer's mate Charlie Read and others, he knew that Billy would be taken care of by experts. Apart from the few scratches, bruises and the back of one hand which hurt like hell, he had been lucky - which was more than could be said for Tommy Stock. 'The bastard deserved it' he murmured to himself, taking consolation in the one part of the operation that had gone according to plan.

When he was sitting in the back of the police car, where he had been dumped unceremoniously after being handcuffed roughly by the two detective sergeants, his thoughts automatically led to Johnny Spencer. The more he thought about the evening's events, the more he thought that Spencer had to be behind the timely arrival of the law. They had been set up - he was sure of that - and if Wilson had had anything to do with it he would find out from inside the nick and deal with him. There would be no mistake about that.

Whether Vic Steadman would be the same force, inside prison or out, without brother Billy to protect him and do his dirty work, remained to be seen.

# CHAPTER TWENTY-EIGHT

Johnny had been waiting for about half an hour in the main passenger departure lounge at Heathrow Airport when Claire arrived. She was alone. 'Trust her to be independent' thought Johnny, although secretly it was one of her qualities that he most admired. Her cases were piled up on one of the little yellow and brown airport trolleys. He hurried forward to help her.

She was dressed in a smart beige suit, with white blouse and matching shoes. Her dark hair, loose and raven, stood out in contrast to the beige. She looked a picture and the lines of worry, which were all too apparent the last time they had met, had gone. She seemed much more relaxed and her cheeks were slightly flushed with the excitement of the journey which lay ahead.

'I must be mad to let this girl go' thought Johnny, as he kissed her lightly on the cheek. It was warm and tasted good.

'Hi, Claire' he said softly.

'Hello, Johnny' she replied easily.

'You look terrific and much more relaxed than the last time I saw you.'

'Yes, I feel much better, now that I am finally on my way' she paused and said 'Can we have a coffee and a talk somewhere, Johnny?'

'Sure, let's check-in your luggage and we'll take it from there.'

He took charge of the trolley and found the check-in desk for the flight to New Zealand. Claire dealt with the documentation while Johnny loaded the luggage on to the conveyor belt. He laughed at her having to pay for excess baggage.

'It's all I have in the world, you know' she said anxiously.

She nodded and checked her watch, saying 'Can we have that coffee then? There's only about half an hour before I'll be called.'

Making their way to the self-service cafeteria, they were soon facing each other across a table sipping their coffee, each deep in thought. Johnny waited, feeling that she had something she was anxious to ask him.

'Johnny – Claire'

They had both spoken at the same time and they laughed as each said 'Go on' simultaneously again.

'Johnny' said Claire finally, in a serious voice 'You must have heard about my brothers. Vic's on a murder charge and Billy's an accessory, likely to spend goodness knows how long in a prison hospital. The doctors say he may spend the rest of his life in a wheelchair.'

'Claire, I ...'

'No, don't interrupt, just listen' she insisted 'Don't worry, I haven't got any sympathy for them. They deserve all they get. No, what I wanted to know was ...' She paused and looked deeply into his eyes '... did you know it was all going to happen. Did you know anything at all about it. Because ever since I've known you my life had been turned upside down and full of tragedy. Why? Why, Johnny?' her voice rose and she glanced around, embarrassed in case anyone had overheard.

Johnny reached across the table and took both her hands in his 'Claire I can't deny that I've been involved, but none of it was intended - it was just a chain reaction, I assure you. One day, I hope to be able to explain to you fully exactly why.'

He paused, swallowed, and then continued seriously 'Please, please accept that and the fact that I have been very fond of you right from our first meeting in the florist shop.'

Before she could answer, he continued 'Please have this as a little going away present.'

He took a sealed envelope from his inside jacket pocket 'But you have to promise me that you won't open it until you are on that plane and in the air.'

She hesitated, as if she might refuse, but seeing that he was so serious and apparently apologetic, she relented, took the envelope and put it in her handbag.

'Thank you. Sorry I haven't got anything for you.'

'Don't worry about that, all I want is for us to part friends.'

'Well, I do have one thing actually' she replied, reaching into her handbag and also producing an envelope 'It's my address in New Zealand' and she added 'I wasn't sure till now whether I would give it to you or not.' She handed him the envelope.

'Thanks, I'm glad you did. Perhaps I'll be able to make up for all the trouble I've caused you. I sincerely hope so.'

\*\*\*\*\*\*

The flight announcement for Claire's departure came over loud and clear and they got up and made their way slowly to the barrier. 'Goodbye, Johnny' she said, suddenly turning and offering her hand. Her voice broke halfway through. She was still uncertain of him. There were still too many unanswered questions.

He ignored the outstretched hand and, without inhibition, he clasped her to him and kissed her gently on both cheeks. 'Goodbye, look after yourself' he said, as he looked deeply into her eyes, which were half-filled with tears. She turned quickly without another word and was gone.

He stood to one side as the crowd moved forward to be checked through the barrier and watched as she produced her tickets and made her way in the direction of the departure lounge. Her trim figure finally disappeared amongst the other travellers and, without a backward glance, she had gone.

A feeling of emptiness engulfed him and he remained for several minutes staring at the place where he had last seen her. 'Was he a fool to have let her go?' New Zealand seemed a hell of a long way away, although she had said she needed time to recover. Time and space. 'Time is a great healer' he consoled himself with the hackneyed phrase.

Suddenly he was aware of being jostled, as even more passengers arrived for the flight and, still thinking of Claire, he turned and made his way slowly through the mass of travellers of all nationalities. The world seemed to be on the move, a dozen different languages could be heard.

Arriving at the top of the Queen's Building, he breathed deeply, glad to be out in the open once more, and away from all the bustle. His companions turned out to be a mixture of young plane spotters, visitors to London, and people like himself waiting to see the departure of a particular flight.

The big Qantas DC10 was already at the gate and as the passengers, Claire amongst them, boarded the plane, the luggage and various services were being loaded on board. The huge plane then left the stand and taxied to the end of the far runway, the final pre-take off procedures were completed and its mighty jets screamed as the engines were put into full power. Finally, the plane was speeding along the runway, the fat wheels lifted clear and suddenly the nose tipped up, it climbed steeply and, in seconds, was lost in the clouds.

Johnny waved along with the others, some of whom were in tears, so perhaps Claire wasn't the only one leaving the old world behind and seeking a new life on the other side of the world. He imagined he had seen Claire waving from a window seat, but the figure was so small that it could have been anyone.

Inside the plane, Claire actually was sitting in a window seat and she had waved to the people on top of the Queen's

Building, hoping that Johnny was amongst them. She took a handkerchief from her handbag and dried her eyes. Putting the handkerchief away she saw the envelope which Johnny had given her and, with trembling hands, she tore off the top edge and removed the contents. To her astonishment, it turned out to be £5,000 worth of blank American Express traveller's cheques. She could hardly believe her eyes.

'What was going on here? Where on earth had the money come from?'

Checking the envelope again she found a brief note from Johnny, which said simply 'Darling Claire, this money is rightfully yours. Apologies for all the trouble I've caused you. I hope to explain one day, my darling. Love, Johnny.'

She crushed the letter in her hands and for several minutes remained stunned and confused.

Unknown to her a similar amount had been donated anonymously to the Police Station Fund set up for the widow and family of Albert Thompson.

After much deliberation and heart searching, Johnny had decided that the money should be shared equally between Albert's widow and family and Claire, the people who had suffered most from all the grief and upheaval since he had started on his revenge trail. Poor old Smithy had no one to worry about him.

He made his way down the steps of the Queen's Building with mixed feelings. On the one hand, he was pleased to have brought his investigations to a successful conclusion as far as the people he cared for were concerned. This had been at the expense of old Smithy, Claire's father and Tommy Stock, although in Stock's case it was probably poetic justice. On the other hand, he couldn't get Claire out of his mind and he tried to picture her opening the letter and wondered what her reaction would be.

'Was he a fool to have let her go?' He had genuinely enjoyed her company, as much as any woman since the early days of his marriage.

Reaching his cab, he slid into the front seat and started the engine. As he pulled the seat belt across his body, the envelope which Claire had given him crackled. He patted the pocket and smiled to himself. New Zealand wasn't all that far away.

He eased the car into first gear, put in the clutch and headed towards London.   Back to 'the Smoke'.

www.ingramcontent.com/pod-product-compliance
Lightning Source LLC
Chambersburg PA
CBHW031113030726
47496CB00002BA/515